THE THERAPIST

C.L. SUTTON

PROLOGUE

*T*he weight of my father's casket was nothing compared to the burden of the mess he's left behind.

The atmosphere in my living room is thick with grief. It sticks to my
skin like a fog of misery. Mourners turn to me with expectation in their
eyes, waiting for me to cut through the tension.

I clear my throat, grabbing a moment to gather my thoughts. There's
plenty I want to say, but I have no energy for the truth. I'm raw.

It's just easier to lie.

'Thank you all for coming today.' To my relief, my voice sounds
steadier than I feel. 'This is a very sad occasion. For all of us. My dad was
an exuberant character who touched many lives and his death has hit us
incredibly hard. But I'd like to think of today as a celebration, too. You
all knew Dad as a terrific man, a caring friend, and a loving husband.
We should be grateful to have had him in our lives, and we should rejoice
in that today. Let's raise a glass to the big guy.'

Everyone raises their drinks in the air. 'To Graham,' they chant. A
chorus of ignorance.

I scan the room, taking in the sea of faces, some familiar, others less so. That so many are here to pay their respects is a testament to my father's ability to manipulate. If they knew the real Graham, my home would be empty.

The mourners settle back into their conversations and approach the buffet table, while I take a minute to breathe. The wine I've been sipping suddenly feels like acid in my stomach and I rush to the downstairs toilet to escape the heavy atmosphere and sympathetic glances. The loo is nestled under the stairs and the space is tiny around my large frame. I loosen my tie, undo the top button of my pristinely ironed shirt, and allow myself to breathe deeply. Voices sound inches from the other side of the door and I pull the lock across, feeling my shoulders relax at the certainty that I am truly alone, if only for a moment.

I look in the mirror and do not recognise the man looking back at me. My usually perfect posture is drooping, weighed down by recent trauma. The deep shadows under my blue eyes resemble bruising, and I look so much older than my forty-two years of age. I practise the smile for my guests outside and it looks tired and insincere. I force it harder, showing more of my straight white teeth, but I'm just too tired. The smile slips away.

I can't do this.

I splash cold water on my face. The shock of the chill on my skin pulls my attention from recent events and I force myself to focus on the here and now. I just need to get through today. Six deep breaths. In through the nose, out through the mouth. 'I can do this,' I say to my reflection. I don't believe a word of it, but I feel calmer nevertheless. If only my reflection revealed the same.

As I leave the toilet, I immediately catch sight of my mother across the living room. She looks more frail than I've ever seen her, tiny and ghost-like. Her once vibrant eyes are now dimmed with sorrow, and her face is pale and drawn. Her gaunt cheeks practically stop my pulse. She dabs at her damp cheeks with a tissue as she gazes wistfully out the bay window.

As if she senses me watching her, she spins to look at me. Her eyes are like stone. She motions me over and I obey. She reaches out to take my hand and gives it a little squeeze. Her skin feels like creased tissue paper. I resist the urge to pull away.

'That was a lovely speech,' she says, her voice barely above a whisper.

I shrug off the compliment. 'It was only a few words.'

A smile flickers across her face as she surveys the room. 'Well, it seems to have worked.'

I follow her gaze, noticing how the atmosphere has indeed lightened. Jackets have been removed, now draped over the backs of chairs, and the once sombre faces now wear expressions of fond remembrance as people share stories of my father and catch up with long-forgotten friends.

I pull my hand away. 'I can't do this, Mum.'

She breathes in deeply like she wants to say something, but the words fall away before materialising. She just shakes her head at me. "Well, you have to push everything aside, Zack. You can manage a couple more hours. Do it for me, darling. It's been a hard day for me, too.'

I cannot imagine what she's going through. Losing your husband of over forty years must feel like losing a part of yourself. Then to top it off, she has just had her own soul torn in two. But she's strong as an ox. She'll be okay. She has to be, because I can't hold her up right now.

I'm realising that I never really knew my mum. There has always been a colossal distance between us. I always assumed that Dad's love had wedged itself between us, creating a chasm that we just couldn't stitch together. Don't get me wrong, I love my mother and I know she loves me. I'm just not sure how I can ever really foster a bond.

'This is killing me,' I confess, but Mum's eyes are flitting around the room, distracting me.

'Where is she now?' she asks.

'Who?' I ask stupidly. I know exactly who she means. It's a poor attempt at forcing away the question.

'Your wife.'

I scowl. I hate that word. I hate everything about that woman. 'She's gone.'

Mum just nods. 'That's probably for the best?'

I take a step backwards, unsure what to say next. Is Mum right? Is it better if my wife and I just sever ties? Shouldn't I put up more of a fight? How am I supposed to figure out the answer when there blatantly isn't one?

A tall man wearing a bowler hat comes over and greets Mum with a tight squeeze, so I take my opportunity to escape. I fend off people coming at me with condolences and questions regarding my wife's whereabouts. I can feel my breath thickening in my lungs and an insane urge to scream it out of me.

'Everything all right?' I turn to see my younger brother, Aaron, his blue eyes narrow as he takes me in.

The shadows under his eyes are more prominent than mine, which is saying something. We share the same deep brown hair colour, but Aaron's is in desperate need of a cut and greys litter his hairline. His grief is far more potent than mine and it's written all over his face.

He's picking at a scab on his chin where he's screwed up shaving, and I notice his nails need cutting. In fact, looking at him more carefully, he looks like he just needs a good wash. I feel for him. He's been through a lot, too, only instead of the sudden shock I have experienced of late, Aaron has been suffering his entire life.

As much as I want to love my brother, I just don't know how. The pain runs too deep.

'I'm fine,' I say through gritted teeth.

But Aaron's expression is unreadable. 'I don't believe you.' His tone is sincere, but I shrug him off. 'Where's Sarah?' he asks. Her name grates on me and I fight the urge to shudder. Aaron's friendship with my wife has always put me on edge and now I wonder how privy he is to my situation.

I clench my jaw. 'She couldn't make it.'

'Really? She was at the service though. And her and Dad were really close.'

'Yeah, well, sometimes things aren't just about Dad.'

Aaron looks me up and down with creased eyebrows. He may be the younger brother, but he towers over me and is probably twice as wide, having never lost the bulk gifted to him by his former life as a soldier.

I clench my jaw and change the subject. 'Surprised you made it.' Something unpleasant gnaws at my stomach. Pain, guilt, anger? All of the above.

He meets my gaze, his sunken eyes boring into mine. 'I couldn't miss it. It felt wrong. And it'd kill Mum not to have us both here. She deserves better than that.'

Memories of the last time I saw Aaron haunt me. A darkness surrounds me and I avert my gaze. 'I can't do this,' I say, to no one in particular.

Aaron looks as done with all this as I am. His shoulders sag, his jaw twitches, and his eyes flicker between me and the door like he wants to run away. We make small talk about nonsense, getting us nowhere. We're still in pain, we're still awkward, and we still hate our father.

After what feels like an eternity, Aaron turns and stalks off into the kitchen, his shoulders rigid with barely-contained grief. I force out the breath I've been holding and with Herculean effort, plaster yet another smile on my face. I can't let the cracks start to show. I can't reveal the pain that rips through me. If I slip for even a second, I might just crack in two. No, my mask has to stay in place, no matter how much it hurts.

I know I have work to do with Aaron. We need to rebuild our relationship from scratch and I pray we can do that. I just don't know how deep Dad's lies run. It's something I have to focus on when my head is clearer. Everything feels muffled right now, like I'm wearing huge headphones to block out the noise of my anguish.

I glance around the room, avoiding eye contact with the crowd. Dad's cheerful face catches my eye and I walk over to the photo sitting on the bookshelf. I pick it up and look at the man who raised me. He's looking straight at the camera with a huge smile on his face – a picture of health. One arm is draped over Mum's shoulders, the other hand placed on my wife's shoulder whilst I stand on Sarah's other side, smiling in blissful ignorance. Aaron is nowhere to be seen. He wasn't invited that day.

'I hope you rot in hell, Dad,' I mutter.

CHAPTER 1

BEFORE

The second I walk through the door, my mood drops. Gone is the lightness I felt after a productive day at work. Now, I just feel dread.

I never know what I will face behind the door. Is it the bearable version of the woman I married? Or have I got a fight on my hands? I hope it's the former. I always hope it's the former. There's no way to win a fight with Sarah. She's impossible. I have never heard her admit fault and it drains me to be "wrong" all the time.

I step into the hall and untie my laces before stacking my shoes on the rack and placing my bag in the cupboard. The house is quiet. There's no drawl of cartoons in the living room, no music blaring down the stairs. Silence doesn't bode well.

I head into the living room. An empty bottle of wine rests on the coffee table, and I scoop it up and take it to the recycling box in the kitchen. Crumbs litter the work surface, and a butter knife has been left out, mustard smeared across the marble top. Tutting, I grab a cloth and work at removing the stain. It won't come off.

I can sense her behind me before I hear her, but I ignore her, preferring not to engage sooner than I need to. It isn't until she coughs that I turn to acknowledge her.

'Sarah,' I mutter. Barely a greeting.

'Zack,' she returns, with a smile on her lips. She's trying to act nice, but we both know she likes to play with me and as hard as I try, I can't help but let it bother me. I have played her game for years.

She stands there watching me clean her mess, clutching a half-drunk glass of wine. She brings the rim of the glass to her lips whilst maintaining eye contact with me, but doesn't take a sip. She's taunting me. She knows I hate how much she drinks.

Sarah claims to only drink when Georgia is either in bed or out, but current circumstances suggest otherwise.

Biting, I ask, 'Where's Georgia?' The mustard stain I've been scrubbing at finally fades to nothing. I throw the cloth into the sink and brush breadcrumbs into my hand to drop them into the bin.

After a long day at work, I always long to hold my daughter's timid frame in my arms so that she feels safe. Her gangly limbs feel so fragile wrapped in mine and her big brown eyes are full of innocence. She needs my protection at all costs.

'At a mate's house. She'll be back soon.'

A sigh escapes me before I can stop it.

'What?' she asks, her eyes narrowing.

'Nothing, Sarah.' I can see she's in the mood for a fight and I need to tread carefully here. If Georgia is coming home soon, I can't have her walking in on us arguing. Again.

'No – what were you sighing at?' she snaps.

I squeeze my eyes shut. 'I didn't sigh,' I tell her, whilst sighing.

'No – go on – tell me what you're thinking. I know you're thinking something bad about me, as per usual. And seeing as you're such a *decent* man, the decent thing to do would be to tell me the truth.' Her voice is full of sarcasm. It's like fingernails on a chalkboard.

Fuck it. I'm tired of holding back all the time. Sometimes, Sarah needs the cold hard truth. Maybe it's the only way I can get her to change. I tell her, 'I'm just not surprised that Georgia is at a friend's house. You're always passing her off on other people.'

Her cheeks tinge red, and she downs the rest of her drink. 'That's utter bollocks! You know I dote on that girl. If Georgia wants to hang out with a friend, then I am more than happy to oblige. It's good for her to develop friendships.' She steps towards me, and I step back to avoid the spittle flying out of her mouth. 'And I thought psychology was supposed to be your thing.'

Oh, shit. I woke the bitch.

I try to backtrack. 'I know, Sarah. I shouldn't doubt you. I'm just tired.'

'Doubt me? You do nothing *but* doubt me! You go out of your fucking way to make me look like a bad mother!' She's yelling now and I'm backed into the corner of the unit, leaving me nowhere to escape her jabbing index finger.

I don't know when our marriage disintegrated. We didn't exactly start off as the happy lovey-dovey couple the movies like to make out is the norm. But, I still always assumed our feelings would deepen and our love would grow.

But that never happened. I have thought about leaving so many times, but I know that no judge would grant me custody of our little girl, and I cannot bear to have Georgia live with Sarah alone. It would kill me to lose my little girl.

So, here we are. Trapped in a miserable marriage with an unhappy daughter. It breaks my heart.

Sarah is still ranting when I refocus my attention to the present. 'We both know what you think about me, but you're *wrong*, Zack. Wrong! I am a good mother!'

'Mummy?' Georgia's sweet voice injects into Sarah's tantrum, and her anger fizzles out immediately. She has the good grace to look ashamed as she spins around to pull Georgia in for a hug.

For a six-year-old, Georgia is incredibly perceptive. I guess that's what being raised by parents who hate each other does to you. She's standing in the doorway now, looking so small and vulnerable. I flash Georgia a smile as she accepts Sarah's embrace with no reciprocation. She's clutching Hugsy, her stuffed bear, to her pinafore dress. She's been carrying Hugsy around since she learnt how to clutch her little hands. I know she should have let go of her crutch by now, but he's her strongest ally in this war. I feel so guilty to see her pull him close to her chest as she eyes Sarah and me with fear.

'Hey, beautiful. Good day at school?' I ask her, reaching into the pantry for a packet of crisps. I walk over to her and hand her the Quavers, planting a kiss on her forehead.

As I edge closer to the two of them, my close proximity repels my wife away from me. She goes to put her now empty glass in the dishwasher, but we both know she'll top up another glass within the hour.

There's a brief pause as Georgia eyes us and tries to find the courage to talk. 'School was good! Mrs Mitchell says I am ready to move into the red group for reading and writing.' She smiles at me and my heart swells with pride. 'I've learnt all the blue words now.'

'Yeah? That's great news! The red group is the hardest group, right? You must be super clever. Like your dad.'

She giggles, a high-pitched noise that makes me swoon. 'No, Daddy. Purple is the top group. Red is before that one.'

Sarah huffs behind me, pleased at my mistake.

'Oh, yeah,' I tell Georgia, ruffling her hair. 'I knew that.'

Georgia scampers off into the living room and moments later, the irritating sound of Bluey's high-pitched voice filters into the kitchen. The atmosphere is once again dense with hate.

'She's a good kid,' I say to Sarah, in a desperate attempt at a truce. Georgia is the only thing we can agree on.

'Yeah,' Sarah nods, opening the fridge and pulling out a new bottle of pinot grigio. 'She is a good girl. Despite everything.'

CHAPTER 2

As I head into work the next day, I'm still reeling.

After Sarah drank the second bottle of wine last night, she cried. Not the ladylike, sweet cry of a woman in distress. It was the deep wail of a drunk. Thankfully, Georgia slept through the whole tirade, but the sound of Sarah's cries made every single one of my muscles tense and my anger boil, so I didn't sleep a wink. Of course, Sarah snoring her head off at four in the morning in her bedroom next to mine did nothing to improve my mood. Finally, having to get up an hour early to finish my work from the previous day turned my mood from bad to thunderous.

I'm worried it will rub off on my clients if I don't shake it off, so when I enter the office I plant a smile on my face to chase away my annoyance. My receptionist, Chelsea, looks at me with concern. Her long nails cease tapping on the keyboard, providing a welcome relief from the tip-tap of acrylic on plastic.

'Are you okay, Dr Briens?' she asks, cocking her head.

I smile at her with as much warmth as I can muster. Chelsea doesn't deserve my emotional baggage. I'm here to listen to problems, not dish them out. 'I'm fine, just a little tired. I brought some treats!' I set down the box of pink iced doughnuts on her desk and her eyes light up.

'You do know how to brighten up the midweek blues, Dr Briens!'

I chuckle. 'Blues? Are you not happy working here, Chelsea?' I tease. I know she's happy here. Chelsea has been working for me for over a year now and she is exceptionally competent and generously recompensed for it. I don't know where I would be without her.

'Oh, no, I didn't mean it like that!' she gasps.

'I know, I know. Relax. We all get the midweek blues sometimes. Even those who are amazing at their job.'

She bats her ridiculously long eyelashes at me. 'Thank you, Dr Briens.' A hint of rosiness appears under her makeup, and she gets up to take the doughnuts into the tiny kitchen behind her desk. 'I'll put the kettle on,' she calls out as the door shuts behind her.

I stroll into my office and feel the usual sense of pride as I cast my eyes over the space. My anger hangover washes away as I breathe in the scent of wood from my ostentatious desk that sits in the middle of the room. I didn't need to get such a big desk, but when I opened the practice five years ago, buying an extravagant piece to work from felt like the ultimate celebration.

The files I am clutching under my arm drop heavily onto my leather swivel chair, and I head over to the window to watch the world go by until Chelsea brings me my morning coffee. People-watching is a habit of mine. I love to imagine where people are heading and where they're rushing from. I like to picture their homes, their families, and their professions. It's fun. My office sits above the busiest bank in town, so there's always a plethora of people on the street in a full variety of shapes, sizes, and backgrounds. It's a nosy man's haven. I tug on the curtain to straighten it out.

There's a light tap on my door and Chelsea appears, holding my favourite mug, the black coffee leaving a trail of steam in its wake. She places the cup neatly in the centre of the coaster on my desk.

'Thank you, Chelsea. As soon as my first client arrives, please tell her I'm free to see her.'

Chelsea gives me a small smile and nods, before heading back to her desk to answer the ringing phone, closing my door behind her.

Ten minutes later, my door opens slowly, and Miss Reeves pops her head around the doorframe. She looks afraid. I stand to welcome her, careful not to approach too quickly or get too close, in case I startle her.

'Come in, Miss Reeves.' I gesture at the sofa in the corner. I tried to make the corner as welcoming as possible, but it was Chelsea's feminine touch that turned the space from welcoming to cosy. Her additions of a throw on the sofa and plants on the side tables were the perfect finishing touches.

Miss Reeves takes a seat at the far side of the sofa while I sit on the armchair opposite, giving her ample personal space. 'Please call me Fiona,' she mumbles, her eyes everywhere but on mine. She spots the row of fiction books nestled in the shelves amongst the educational volumes. 'You like *Harry Potter*?' she asks with surprise.

I tap my pen on the pad of paper resting on my knee. 'Guilty as charged,' I laugh. 'Everyone needs a little magic in their life.'

Her shoulders visibly relax, and I settle deeper into my chair.

'This is your first time in therapy, Fiona?'

She nods. 'My GP persuaded me to come. She said it'll help the anxiety meds work better.'

I click my pen and make a note. 'Yes and no,' I admit. 'Therapy won't impact the medication you're taking, but it will help get to the root of the problems. Sometimes, the meds are required to make you strong enough to pull at the weeds. And the weeds need pulling before we can plant a new garden. That's where I come in.'

She smiles a smile that lights up her entire face.

Six months ago, Chelsea suggested she have a pre-meeting chat with each client to glean what they're like as a person, and I must say, her plan has unlocked a new level of therapy. Chelsea's notes described Fiona as a fan of *Harry Potter* and an avid gardener. By making small tweaks to the environment and honing my approach to the conversation, a whole new level of trust opens up. I can already feel Fiona warming to me and her tension evaporating.

'Just some ground rules before we start. I find it best to get the admin out of the way so we can shift our focus onto you without interruption.' I place my pen on my notepad. 'You are welcome to make however many appointments you like – I am here for you. If you need an urgent appointment, let Chelsea know. I have set hours put aside every day for those who need them at short notice.'

Fiona nods, leaning forward to take in my every word. I imagine she hasn't felt someone want to help her like this in a long time.

'I'm sure you can imagine, I can't take calls out of hours. I can't meet outside the office either. It's for your protection. This office is your safe space. Whatever you say in here, stays in here. I will not alert the authorities without your consent.' I hand her an information pack that I give to every client. 'Should you need help, whether it's someone to talk to, or somewhere to stay, all the information in there is tested and trusted. There's help for you out there, Fiona. And hopefully the work we do in here will give you the courage to extend your hand and ask for it.' Fiona nods and clutches the information to her chest like she's holding a bible. 'I can email you the same information if you can't have hard copies in your home.'

Her eyes say it all. There's a fear there that hurts me deeply every single time I see it. Fiona is worn down and broken, but if you look closely enough, you can see the woman she used to be. The vivacious, confident woman she deserves to be now.

We'll get her back. Together. It's why I love what I do.

'You hinted on the phone that you're having a hard time letting go of your partner?' I ask her.

'That's right,' she stammers. 'Phil died. He's gone. But I miss him. You know?'

'And how do you feel about missing him?'

She wobbles her head at me, her lips pressed together. 'It's just … stupid.'

'So, you feel you shouldn't miss him, is that right? It sounds like there is a conflict with your emotions here?'

Her eyes widen. 'That's exactly it! Everyone keeps asking me how I can miss someone who treated me like that. I don't know what the hell is wrong with me.'

I press my lips together and place my pen down again. 'There's nothing wrong with you, Fiona. I think we need to step back a little before we can move forward. Let's go back. Tell me about your relationship with Phil.'

An hour later, Fiona stands to shake my hand. Tears have stained her cheeks with crusty salt, but her eyes look less burdened by the pain of her past.

She holds my hand a little longer than I'd like and for a second I worry she's going to hug me. I drop my hand. Too much physical contact is a dangerous step to cross with someone so vulnerable, especially as someone in a perceived role of authority. I know the dangers of my profession.

'Same time next week?' I ask her.

'Oh, yes, definitely.' She bustles out with a cheery wave to Chelsea, who calls out a friendly goodbye. Fiona leaves a different woman than the one who walked in, and I enjoy the familiar sense of pride that comes with my job.

After asking Chelsea to put the kettle on, I drop into the seat behind my desk to type up my notes on Fiona's case. I hate this part. I have a keen eye for detail and a strong urge for accuracy, so this always takes much longer than I'd like it to. However, it's also a good time to reflect. I don't like to decide on a treatment plan when I'm mid-conversation with a client, in case I miss a nuance or key detail that shines light on their situation.

Leaving my previous role at the hospital was a ballsy move. My colleagues mocked me and said I'd be back within six months because no one wants to pay for therapy. But here I am, proving all of them wrong.

Choosing to specialise in helping victims of domestic abuse was no easy feat. Abused women (and sometimes men) aren't the most open about their troubles. Sadly, most don't even view their circumstance as a problem that needs professional help. They feel like they're the ones in the wrong; like they *deserve* the abominable treatment dished out by the person who allegedly loves them.

I cast my mind back to Miss Reeves – Fiona. The abuse she suffered at the hands of the man who supposedly loved her was never physical. But when you have lost all sense of identity, all self-confidence, and everyone close to you, the control is a prison. And the neglect? Torture.

It's no wonder Fiona wasn't able to look me in the eye.

But I'm confident I can fix things for her. I can help her dig herself out of that horror show.

Chelsea brings me my coffee as I am staring into space, thinking about how I can help this woman rediscover her sense of self. Chelsea has a cheeky smile on her face. She's up to something. 'Everything okay?' I ask with comic suspicion.

Her eyes light up. 'You still haven't noticed, have you?'

I frown and glance around the room. What decor has she sneaked in now? She giggles, drawing my attention to her, and she presses her hand to her chin. 'Hmm, I wonder what it could be,' she says, tapping a finger against her bottom lip. A finger weighed down by the biggest rock I have ever seen.

'Chelsea! Congratulations!'

She squeals in a way that makes me wince. I don't like loud noises. 'He asked me last night! In Whitestone Park.'

I raise my eyebrows. Whitestone Park is well-known for its amazing children's playground and as a nighttime haunt for homeless drug addicts. Hardly a spot for a romantic gesture.

As if reading my mind, Chelsea blushes. 'It's where he took me for our first date. We had a picnic by the lake. It was romantic!' She practically pleads, batting her false lashes at me.

I hold my hands up. 'You don't have to explain it to me. It sounds lovely.' I try to inject my voice with sincerity, but being married to Sarah has ripped all sense of romance out of me. I wouldn't know a romantic gesture if it hit me in the face.

Chelsea squeals again, holding her glittering finger to her chest. 'I just can't wait to start our lives together. It's like I have been waiting for this all my life, you know? Someone to devote myself to. Someone to declare my love to for the rest of my life.' She looks up wistfully and I have to resist the urge to roll my eyes into the back of my head. I don't want to appear cruel.

Thankfully, Chelsea's phone shrills before I have to feign more delight, and she goes to pick it up. 'I'll put the date of the wedding in your calendar once we decide on one.' She winks as she looks back at me over her shoulder.

I couldn't think of anything worse right now.

CHAPTER 3

The weekend rolls around at a slow pace and the prospect of spending time with my family always fills me with that sense of joy that only familiarity can provide.

My parents' house sits right in the heart of the vast surrounding countryside. It's a palatial brick monument to my dad's successful investments in the stock exchange. As a boy, I never really understood Dad's methods of making money. And as an adult, I still don't understand. Financial investments have never been my thing. I prefer to invest in myself.

Mum answers the door with charming gusto and leads me and Georgia into the kitchen, where I welcome the warmth from the AGA. The smell of baked bread makes my mouth water and flour is still scattered over the work surface as Mum kneads another batch of dough.

'Your dad is outside, darling. By the pond.' Mum ushers me outside into the back garden. 'Can you go and fetch him? He'll be cold.' She places the ball of dough in a bowl and rinses her hands before turning to Georgia and pulling her in for a hug. 'Fancy a drink, honey?' she asks her.

I head across the grounds towards the lake Mum likes to refer to as a "pond". In my opinion, if you need a boat to get across, it's definitely a lake. A mansion in the countryside always felt repulsive to me. The surrounding fields smell of cow shit and the weekly housekeeping bill is more than what I pay in tax. Very ostentatious. Very unnecessary. I much prefer my sensible house in town; large, but practical. Modern and stylish.

But, each to their own.

I step over a puddle of mud, but brown slop oozes over my shoe anyway, and I grit my teeth with frustration. I add "clean shoes" to my mental to-do list.

Dad is sitting in his usual place on the bench, watching over the koi weaving around the reeds. His plaid shirt is pulled tight over his stomach, the buttons clinging on for dear life should his gut suddenly burst through. He's hunched over like he has the weight of the world on his shoulders, and I am saddened to see him bring a cigarette to his lips. After years of promising to quit smoking, we've all had to accept that it's never going to happen.

'Dad!' I call over as I approach him, making him jump.

'Jesus Christ, Zack. You gave me a heart attack there.' He stubs out his cigarette on the bench, raises an arm for a hug, and I embrace him. 'I wasn't expecting to see you today. Everything okay?'

'We needed to get out of the house and Georgia wanted to see her Nan and Pops.'

His beaming smile showcases his wrinkles. 'Georgia's here? Why didn't you say so?' He pushes himself off the bench and stomps back towards the house.

I try not to grumble. If the silly idiot kept his phone on him, it would have saved me the walk over here and I wouldn't have muddied my brogues. I follow him, watching him slowly lumber ahead.

'How's it going?' he asks me, his breathing already laboured from the stroll. I gather he hasn't been working on the walking plan I sent him.

'Oh, you know, working hard as always.'

He smiles at me, but it's more like a grimace, as if he's in pain. Dad's always been proud of my work ethic. I feel like I'm the only son he can be proud of. 'And how's that gorgeous wife of yours?'

I press my lips tightly together, careful of Dad seeing me. Dad has always had a soft spot for Sarah. I don't know why. He sees her as a beautiful, well-put-together mother, refusing to believe she's the hot mess she actually is. 'Yeah, she's okay,' I lie.

Dad chuckles. 'You're not a very good liar, Zack. What's going on?'

I struggle to tell Dad what's wrong in a way that doesn't make me look like I'm bitching about my wife. 'It's fine, Dad. Sarah was in a bit of a bad mood this morning, so we thought we'd give her some space.'

'What did you do to piss her off?' The twinkle in his eyes tells me he's making fun, but the question still cuts deep.

'Nothing!' I bite. 'I still can't figure out how I upset her this morning. Maybe I breathed in the wrong direction.'

Dad stops walking to look at me. His cheeks are ruddy, and his eyes look moist from the strain of walking up the gentle slope to his house. 'Oh, Zacharia, don't be so down in the dumps. Everyone has the right to a bit of time to themselves sometimes. And your mum and I are always pleased to see you, anyway.'

My damn father always sees the best side of Sarah. He just doesn't understand.

I see Georgia bouncing around inside the kitchen, and I decide I don't want to get into this now. 'I don't want to talk about it, Dad. Can we just leave it?' My marriage is a constant source of concern to me; it's not fair to pass that concern onto my father.

He stops walking and turns to face me. He looks stern, making me feel like a fourteen-year-old boy again. 'No, we cannot. If there are problems in your marriage, you need to sort them out straight away. Never let things fester. It'll just inject more problems into your home faster than you can say *divorce*, and you don't want that.'

I cringe. I daren't tell him a divorce is what I want more than anything, but I'm just too scared to lose it all. My daughter, my house, my business. Sarah will take everything. 'Dad, please. I can't do this right now ...'

'No, son, listen to me. You think me and your mum have had it plain sailing? Of course not. I bet there's not a single couple on the planet who haven't had problems, but you work through them if you want your marriage to survive. You've been here before and come through the other side. You will this time, too.'

As he's speaking, I can hear his frustration creep up a notch. My father feels very passionate about the sanctity of marriage, and I am fed up with hearing this lecture every time we meet. He knows nothing about what I'm going through.

'Do you hear me?' he pleads.

I nod and continue walking back to the house. We walk the last few steps in silence, only the sound of Dad's gasps and birdsong breaking through the quiet. It's certainly peaceful here.

As we step onto the patio area, I bend down and wipe the tops of my shoes with a rogue tissue I found in my pocket.

Dad chuckles, shaking his head. 'You never change, do you, son? Always ignoring your problems by distracting yourself with shit.'

I shrug, trying not to let my annoyance show. 'What's wrong with cleanliness? A little order never hurt anyone?'

'Ah, but some dirt is good for you, lad. Builds character and strengthens your immune system – or so they say.'

'Pops!' Georgia comes hurtling through the double doors and leaps into his arms. Dad lifts her above his head and swings her around with surprising ease. It takes me back to my youth when Dad would lift me above his head and throw me around like I was a flying Superman. Warmth rushes through me.

He puts Georgia down and lets her lead him into the kitchen, clutching her hand as she rabbits on about a game she's into on the iPad. Dad nods along like he understands, but his raised eyebrows evidence his confusion. I chuckle quietly to myself. Mum already has a cafetiere waiting for us and I gratefully pour myself a mug of coffee before passing the pot to Dad who does the same.

'So, darling girl. How are you doing?' Dad asks Georgia, pulling her onto his knee.

Mum places a plate of biscuits in the middle of the table and Georgia makes a grab for it. I gently pull the plate out of her reach. 'Hang on a minute, young lady. How many of those have you had already?'

'Oh, come on now, Zack. One more won't hurt,' Mum tells me with a sparkle in her eye.

I relent and push the plate back towards Georgia. She takes three biscuits before I have a chance to change my mind. My parents laugh at her cheek, and I can't help but laugh along with them.

Being here makes me realise how difficult it is to exist in my own home. There's a tension in my house that sticks to me even when I leave it, but walking through the door to my parents' home washes all of that away.

We talk about Georgia's school – about how her teacher gave her a sticker for her maths skills, and about her friend Henry who got told off for calling a girl in the year above a "butthead".

'And how's your mum?' Dad asks Georgia now. If he wasn't so huge – and my father – I would have probably confronted him. I know exactly what he's trying to do, and getting Georgia to spill the beans on my marriage is a low blow.

'She's good,' Georgia chirps, but she's a terrible liar. Her cheeks burn crimson and her eyes dart in all directions as she tries to find a way out of the situation.

'Yeah? Where is she today, then? It'd be nice to see her.'

'Dad,' I warn.

Mum's eyes flit between the two of us. She can sense the animosity in the air.

'She's in bed. She's got a hangover,' Georgia admits. 'Again.' She takes another bite of her snack, unaware of the bomb she's just dropped.

Dad turns to me. 'You see? You've got to sort this out. Children pick up on more than you think.'

Dad doesn't need to tell me that. I know exactly what Georgia is aware of. We discussed it in the car on the way over here, and it breaks my heart. I want to wrap Georgia in bubble wrap and whisk her away, but that would put her in even more danger. Fathers always pull the short straw when it comes to custody battles and there's no way in hell I am giving that woman sole access to my child. Georgia will not live under a roof with Sarah without my supervision.

I need everyone to see Sarah for who she truly is before I take on the battle. It's a dire situation, but there's no other option. Dad's dream of me patching things up with Sarah is ludicrous. He's speaking of impossibilities. So, here we are.

The doorbell chimes, cutting through the tense atmosphere, and Mum leaps up to answer it.

Dad leans towards me. 'You're doing a great job with Georgia, you know. She's lucky to have such a devoted father. I just want you to be happy, that's all.'

I swallow hard, suddenly feeling a rush of emotion. 'Thanks, Dad.'

Heavy footsteps sound through the hall. 'It's so nice of you to visit. We haven't seen you in a long time,' Mum trills. I hear my brother grunt in response.

'Uncle Aaron!' Georgia calls out to him as he slinks into the kitchen. Aaron's lost weight. His black jeans are hanging off him and the Guns N' Roses T-shirt he favours so much has a tiny hole in the chest. He looks a mess. I don't understand why he deliberately makes himself look homeless.

'Hey, kiddo,' he says to Georgia, reaching over me for the last biscuit. 'I wasn't expecting to see you here,' he says to me, his tone darkening.

'Why wouldn't you? I'm always visiting. Unlike some.'

'Yeah, well, some of us work two jobs. I don't get the time to swan about.'

'Now, now, boys. No arguing,' Mum says, pulling a can of Coke out of the fridge and handing it to my brother. 'We're so pleased to see you, my darling.' She kisses him on the cheek. 'To what do we owe this pleasure?'

Aaron averts his eyes as he cracks open the can and takes a swig. 'Actually, it's a personal matter,' he says, throwing a glance my way. He pulls out a chair next to mine and sits down heavily.

'We're all family here, Aaron. You can say what you need to say,' Dad says. It's the first thing he's said to him. He never bothered with a greeting.

Aaron glances at me again and shakes his head. 'No, it doesn't matter.'

Dad leans forward. 'What is it, boy? Need more money?'

I look away, unable to stand the atmosphere. Mum takes Georgia by the hand and leads her into the living room.

'No,' Aaron shrugs.

'Of course you do. That's the only reason you ever come here.'

'Dad. Stop,' I say. As much as I agree with Dad's anger, I don't want Georgia to witness more conflict. Aaron might work two jobs, but he never has enough money to fund his life. I don't know when things went so wrong for my little brother.

When Aaron joined the army, we were all so proud. A photo of us standing around a camouflaged Aaron, beaming smiles on all of our faces, still sits on the mantel in the living room. Even Dad put aside his hostility towards Aaron that day. He seemed to feel pride in his youngest son for the first time in his life.

Then, a year into his career, it all crumbled down. Aaron became unrecognisable. He was withdrawn, hating his job, hating us, hating his life. When his commanding officer found marijuana in his room, that was it – game over. I don't think Aaron had ever even tried weed and to this day it still doesn't make any sense to me.

Now, he works as a bouncer at a nightclub in town and sometimes helps a landscaper clear out junk from gardens. My once proud, impressive brother has turned into a man I no longer recognise.

'No, I won't stop,' Dad tells me. 'Not until he sorts himself out.' He glares at Aaron.

'Forget it,' Aaron says, pushing his chair out with a screech and standing up. 'I'll see myself out.'

'Aaron, wait. How much do you need?' I ask him, going to meet him by the door.

He hesitates for a moment, thinking through my offer before gently shaking his head. 'I don't need money,' he says. 'You've got a wife and kid to look after. You don't need to add me to your list.'

'It isn't like that. You're my family, too.'

'Am I?' he asks. Without waiting for a response, he pushes past me and opens the door. Before leaving the house he turns to me and says, 'Because according to Dad, I was out of this family years ago.'

Chapter 4

The morning after my confrontation with Aaron, I arrive at my practice with a knot of tension still lodged in my gut. The office is quiet, the first rays of sunlight just beginning to filter through the blinds as I go through the motions of preparing for the day ahead. I line up my notes parallel to the edge of my desk; I ensure my stapler is full of staples; I plump up the cushions on the sofas.

We'd left my parents' house soon after Aaron stormed out. The confrontation had made Georgia visibly uncomfortable, and Mum was trying far too hard to lift the bad atmosphere that had settled over us. Her shrill tone and overbearing snack distribution started to get on my nerves, so I made our excuses and left.

Aaron needs help. His depression is so advanced that anyone could spot it. And, as a therapist, I am well aware of how much I have let my brother down. Money isn't going to cure his problems. He needs to speak to someone. A professional. I just can't get through to him. And all Dad does is make him feel shit about it.

The ding of the lift pulls me from my thoughts. Chelsea steps onto the floor, her stiletto heels clicking rhythmically against the polished wood. 'Morning, Dr Briens,' she calls out, her voice still tinged with the huskiness of sleep.

I greet her with matching vigour and shut my office door.

I sit and peruse my notes for ten minutes before Chelsea ushers in my first client.

Emily shuffles into my office. Her haunted eyes and hunched shoulders tell me she's experiencing pain. I spy a small bruise on her neck, which she has attempted to cover with makeup. I feel a pull, a yearning to take her pain away.

When I first meet my clients, I am always overcome with a deep desire to help, but there's something about Emily that especially draws me to her. I don't know if it's her angelic features or the depths of anguish in her eyes. My longing to help her is intense and makes my stomach tingle with curiosity.

I offer her a kind greeting and a smile, but she doesn't reciprocate. I gesture at the sofa as I gather my writing materials. She sits down in silence and stares out the window. She bites the inside of her cheek as she enters a deep reflection.

I take my time going over to her so I can take in her presence. There's a charge to the air I cannot explain. It's as if she's a quiet spark about to ignite. Breathing deeply, her chest rises and falls in smooth movements and she occasionally flicks her head to the side to keep her hair out of her face.

I take the armchair across from the sofa, but she doesn't look my way. I clear my throat to draw her attention and say, 'Welcome, Emily. It's a pleasure to meet you.'

She nods, her gaze darting around the room like that of a trapped animal seeking an escape route. I lean back in my chair, granting her space, and I'm immediately regretful. I long for her closeness and pulling away feels painful. I'm drawn to her like a magnet, but I force myself to resist her pull in a bid to maintain professional boundaries.

'This is your first time seeing a therapist?' I ask, keeping my tone carefully neutral.

She nods again, twisting her hands in her lap. I wish she'd talk – I want to hear her voice.

'I imagine you're overwhelmed by all of this, but I just want you to know this is a safe space,' I tell her, my voice low and soothing. 'You are in control here. We can keep the door open, if that would make you more comfortable.'

'Do you record our conversations?' she asks me, looking frightened.

'Only with your permission.'

She thinks carefully before nodding. 'Yes, please.'

I watch as some of the tension evaporates from her shoulders. Clients rarely allow me to record their sessions, so I already see this as a small victory. I beam internally. Emily's decision shows me that she might be ready to make a change in her life. I have a good feeling about this case. I love it when a client comes in ready to make a change, even if they aren't aware of it themselves.

'Would you like to tell me about yourself so we can get to know each other a little better?'

She takes a deep breath and drops her big, blue eyes to the floor. Her cheeks are tinged pink like a doll's. She's utterly beautiful. Her poised posture is perfection. A perfect lady.

'I'll start,' I say gently. 'I'm Dr Zack Briens. I qualified in Psychological and Behavioural Studies at Cambridge and did my master's in Clinical Counselling at Leeds. But that was so long ago.' I smile. 'Then, after working for the NHS for fifteen years, I started my own practice five years ago so I could specifically help victims of abuse.'

Emily doesn't look remotely impressed. Her face remains expressionless. 'I suppose you want to talk about Dexter.' Her voice is low and husky.

'We can leave that for later if you like. Today, I would like very much to hear about *you*. Tell me about yourself, Emily.'

'Millie,' she whispers. 'Call me Millie.'

I smile warmly. 'Certainly, Millie.'

She puffs her chest out and picks at a hole in the knee of her jeans. Her mouth bobs open, but no words come out, so I let her sit in silence whilst she pieces together her thoughts.

I glance at her notes. She's twenty-nine – thirteen years my junior. A broken doll. Her eyes slowly lift to meet mine. They're wide and trusting, and her lips are parted in a silent plea.

'Take your time,' I reassure her. 'Remember, you're in control here.'

Millie blinks at me. 'I nearly didn't come today,' she admits. 'When I booked the appointment, I was in a really bad place; but the last few days have been okay, you know? So, I nearly cancelled.'

I do know. I see it all the time. The cyclic nature of abuse is a constant mental battle for the victim: one minute, they're battered and ready to flee; the next, they feel loved and secure, leaving them to doubt the abuse ever happened. And, in those moments of peace, they believe it will never happen again.

But, it always does.

'What changed your mind? Why did you still come today? If you weren't sure.'

She shrugs. 'I've been through this too many times now. I know how it works.' Her eye contact is now intense, and I shift in my seat. 'I want to be strong enough to leave him. And I need your help.'

I press my lips together and squint at her. 'That realisation is a major step forward, Millie. Most victims never come to that realisation and that's often why so many lose their lives to abuse.'

'I left him already,' she blurts out, like she wants to make me proud. 'A few months ago.'

'Then what happened?' I ask, but I already know the answer.

'I went back to him.'

'Why do you think you did that?'

'Dexter told me he'll change. And he seemed so sure this time. I believed him.'

'What do you think would happen if you left him again – for good?'

Millie's eyes widen. It's a question she's never allowed herself to ask. She's always known she'd go back to him, no matter how many times she left; no matter how long she'd been gone.

She returns to staring out the window whilst she thinks about my question. Eventually, her focus shifts back into the room and she gasps, 'I'd be free!'

Millie's appointment runs long and ninety minutes later, I know all of her hopes and dreams. I have helped to open her eyes to what is out there for her, if only she would dare reach for it. We push past the conversation of her boyfriend; I want her to see that he has no relevance to her future. She can dream without him in her vision.

As the session comes to an end, Millie rises to leave. I shake her hand, allowing my fingers to linger on hers for a fraction too long. I savour the warmth of her soft skin. She flushes a delicate pink and pulls away. I watch her go.

My heart pounds in my chest as the lift doors slide shut behind her. I catch Chelsea's eye as I turn back toward my office, her brow arched in a silent question. I assume she's questioning the lingering handshake and I feel my cheeks burn with shame. I just hope I haven't scared Millie away.

What is wrong with me? I know better than to invade a client's personal space. I turn away and close my office door before heading back to my desk to update Millie's file, the whole time mentally berating myself.

As I type, my mind drifts to the way Millie kept flicking her long, blonde curls over her shoulder. I picture her smooth pink lips revealing pearlescent, straight teeth. Her blue eyes sparkling, despite her pain.

I scowl as I close my laptop. I should refer her to another therapist. I should put some distance between us before this goes any further. But the thought of letting her go, of watching her walk out of my office forever and back into the arms of the man who hurt her, fills me with a cold, clawing dread.

No, I think to myself as I settle back into my chair, my fingers drumming against the smooth leather. Emily needs me. I must help her. I need to see her free of him. And I need to maintain a professional distance. I'm a professional. I can do that.

But doubt has its claws dug into me.

CHAPTER 5

L aughter emanates from the living room as I slip off my shoes. My usual sense of dread at seeing Sarah is lifted when I hear my daughter laughing.

'Stop!' she squeals, her laughter defying her pleas.

I walk in to find Sarah and Georgia tumbling on the rug in the centre of the room. Sarah is tickling Georgia's tummy. Neither has noticed my presence.

'She is telling you to stop,' I say. Despite Georgia's laughter, it's important we teach her consent. Neither hear me and Georgia's squeals amplify.

'Mummy, stop!'

'She is telling you to stop!' I shout over their noisy floor play.

Both turn to look at me with wide eyes and sweat shining on their foreheads. Sarah scowls when she registers me standing just inches away.

'We're having fun,' she says, turning back to Georgia with a smile. The moment has been lost, though. All sense of play has left my daughter, who is better at reading the situation than my adult wife.

'When she says "stop", you must stop. It's important that she learns that.'

Sarah rolls her eyes at me and anger bubbles in my stomach. I take a deep breath in an attempt to remain calm.

'You're not in the office anymore, Zack. And Georgia knows we're just playing, don't you, darling?' We both turn to Georgia who is still lying on her back, panting. She looks like she's about to cry. 'Stop making drama out of nothing.'

'That's enough,' I say, refusing to allow Sarah to drag Georgia into the middle of this. 'You heard what I said. I'm just asking for a little respect.'

I leave the room knowing Sarah will do as I asked. Their joy is gone, and she won't attempt to force it back now Georgia is upset. Sarah's lack of ability to listen to a simple instruction is infuriating. *I* should be teaching Georgia how to behave, not my clueless wife. How dare she defy me when I know best? I'm a qualified psychologist. The entirety of her parenting knowledge comes from Facebook groups for moaning women.

I decide to take a shower to wash away my anger. Sarah has a knack of winding me up, but my mood feels particularly hostile today. Sarah is annoying, but I shouldn't feel this fury. My entire body feels hot and tense, and no amount of time spent under the cool shower clears my pent-up feelings.

Until I arrived home, my day had been excellent. I left my office knowing I have made a difference to five deserving women. Sometimes, my line of work can leave me feeling as battered and bruised as the victims I try to help. Like last year, when a patient didn't attend her session. Upon investigation, I learnt that her ex had finally found her and ended her misery for good by wrapping his fingers around her throat and squeezing every drop of life out of her.

I was sick the night I saw it on the news. Horror stories like that will always impact me, no matter how hard I try to remain objective. And it happens far too often. I tried so hard to heal that poor woman, but I failed. And I still think about her most days; of the ways I could've helped her more.

I don't know what's bothering me now. I can feel the discomfort in the pit of my stomach as I turn off the shower and wrap a towel around my waist.

It's like that feeling you get when you think you've forgotten something, but can't think what it might be. A curious sensation that won't let up.

It's when I look in the mirror that it hits me.

Millie.

When Millie left my office, I felt a strange emptiness. Now she's gone, she's left behind a huge gap. I just can't figure out where this gap has come from and how Millie has opened it up.

It's ludicrous. Millie is a client, and I'm a professional. I put my feelings down to any residual sympathy I have for her situation. But then, Millie's suffering isn't unique. I hear the same stories every damn day. What is it about her?

I cast my mind back to our conversation. Millie spoke with such warm openness, her voice coy, and her demeanour broken. Her words were filled with pain, even the ones she didn't dare speak out loud. Her eyes glistened as they looked into mine, as if she was staring down into the depths of my soul. Her vulnerability awakened my own vulnerabilities, and now I'm left feeling raw. What is it about Millie O'Neale?

I pull on some clean chinos and a polo shirt before heading downstairs. Georgia is now sitting at the dining table, colouring in a picture of Disney princesses. Her tongue pokes out between her lips in concentration. When she sees me her face lights up, all thoughts of Sarah's poor parenting forgotten. 'Daddy, do you like my princess dress?'

I give her picture a cursory glance and smile. 'It's very pink.' The whole picture is coloured in various shades of pink, from the afore-mentioned dress to the crown, to her hair, even the rabbits hopping on the pink grass.

'Pink is my favourite colour,' she announces whilst delving into her pencil case for yet another shade of ... pink. 'Daddy, what's your favourite colour?'

'Grey,' I tell her.

She screws up her nose at me. 'That's a rubbish colour.'

There's a clatter in the kitchen so I walk over to see what mess Sarah is making now. The first thing my eyes land on is an open bottle of wine on the counter. Sarah is squatting on the floor, wrestling a cupboard overflowing with tupperware.

'What's for dinner?' I ask.

She grunts as she pulls out a baking tray. 'Cod.' She stands and shakes out the battered fish from the box. 'And chips.'

My lips purse without my consent.

'Don't look at me like that. You know you're welcome to make dinner for once in your life. Or are you too good to reduce yourself to that level of servitude?'

I scoff. *Servitude.* 'It's dinner, Sarah. You're not being asked to sweep the chimney. Plus, what else do you do around here? You don't work and we have a cleaner come in. Cooking a decent meal is the least you could do for this family.'

'Oh, I think I do more than my fair share!' she seethes. 'I'm still here, aren't I?'

'Only because you have nowhere else to go!'

She leans back against the dishwasher, pressing her hands on the worktop behind her, and stares at me with pure hatred. I can feel the poison of our marriage coursing through her veins.

Why are we doing this to ourselves?

She reminds me: 'You want to be careful what you wish for, Zack. You might just find yourself alone one day.'

I close my eyes, willing Sarah to vanish into thin air, taking all of her baggage with her. Behind my eyelids, Millie's face floats towards me. Her lips lift into a smile that takes my breath away. I can hear Sarah ranting at me, but I brush off her words, letting my fantasy ease me into a happier state. I don't know what it is about Millie that's doing this to me.

But I do know I'm in deep trouble.

CHAPTER 6

The week rolls by in a blur. I avoid Sarah as much as I can and spend some quality time with Georgia, ensuring she knows how much she is loved.

Despite everything our twisted marriage is putting her through, Georgia remains a ray of sunshine – a constant reminder of why I do everything I do; why I cling onto my marriage by my fingertips.

Today, however, brings a new level of excitement. No matter how hard I have tried to distract myself with other cases, my mind keeps returning to Millie. And today, I get to see her again.

I toyed with the idea of cancelling today's appointment to avoid damaging my professional integrity. But I just couldn't do it. What if Millie loses confidence to seek further help? What will happen to her then? No, I can't have that on my conscience.

I hear Chelsea greet Millie in the reception area. I jump up from my desk to stand by the window with my hands behind my back and plant a wistful look on my face. I try to look cool and nonchalant, but by the bashful smile on Millie's lips when she steps inside my office, I can tell I've failed. My cheeks warm with embarrassment.

'Come in and take a seat,' I tell her, but my voice comes out far louder than I intended and the shock of it makes me cough.

'Are you okay, Dr Briens?'

I raise my hand to brush off her concern. 'I'm fine,' I splutter.

She wanders over to the sofa in a graceful movement, and takes a seat closest to my armchair. I hover by the window and watch her run her palms over her tight thighs to straighten her skirt. She crosses one leg over the other, her legs so long I'm unsure how I can sit down without my knees touching hers. As if sensing my gaze, Millie shifts a few inches to the left, her expression still sombre but her eyes now twinkling.

This isn't going to work. I cannot do this. There is no way I can keep a professional distance from this woman. She's magic and her power over me is irresistible. I can't do this. The line between client and therapist is too blurred and it's too much of a risk to carry on. My obsession is dangerous. I sit down and lean back in my chair, searching for the words that will end this torturous relationship.

'Dexter got drunk last night,' she starts. She picks at her thumbnail. 'He's a mean drunk.'

She's gone straight into the session. No warm-up. No preamble. Her confession shocks me back to my senses. I have got to stop making this about me when I have a victim of horrendous abuse who needs my help. It would be selfish to end this now.

'What happened? Did he hurt you?' I usually never ask for specifics of their abuse. If my client wants to relive their trauma, then I will be here to listen, but it's important that I find out whether they're strong enough to talk it through first. I like them to find the strength from within to make the first move, so they can grow that strength and draw on it again and again.

She shakes her head. 'No, I hid in the bathroom with the door locked before he started throwing his fists about,' she whispers. My heart breaks for this woman. She deserves so much better. 'I stayed there until he passed out on the sofa.'

'Oh, Millie,' I breathe. Millie's eyes widen at my lack of professionalism. 'Sorry,' I say. 'I didn't mean it like that. Let's go over what you were thinking when your boyfriend was drunk.'

Millie sits and tells me of her fear, her relief when her boyfriend's temper fizzled out after another few beers, of her hope to be strong enough to leave him for good someday.

'What's holding you back?' I ask her. 'If you know you need to leave, what's keeping you there?'

She takes a deep breath. 'Because he said the next time I leave, he'll kill me.'

***

'I'm just getting some lunch!' Chelsea calls out, zipping up her coat and pulling her bag onto her shoulder. 'Can I get you anything?'

I head over to her with my wallet already in my hand. 'Can you grab me a latte?' I give her a twenty-pound note. 'And your lunch is on me.'

'Best. Boss. Ever!' she drawls, sashaying over to the lift. The doors ping open, and she steps back as my brother barges past her. Chelsea takes his place in the lift and throws me a look of concern. I wave goodbye to reassure her.

I wait for the doors to close and the lift to start its descent before spinning around to face my brother. 'What are you doing here, Aaron?'

He paces the room, running his hand through greasy hair. I watch him with growing impatience. 'Aaron, I've got a client coming in soon.' It's a lie. Mrs Conran cancelled her appointment this morning, but he doesn't need to know that. 'What is it?' I have never seen my brother so agitated. Since being dismissed from the army, he hasn't exactly been easygoing, but today his irritability has stepped up a notch.

Finally, he stops pacing and turns to look at me. His eyes are glassy, and he looks on edge, like he's in the mood to lash out. My office is no place for this man.

'What do you want?' I ask him.

'I need to talk.' I wait, but he doesn't speak.

'Well? Go on, then.'

Aaron sighs and stares down at the floor. All of his pent-up energy evaporates. 'I, erm ... I need money. My landlord is kicking me out.'

I take a deep breath. Why do I get the feeling this is about something other than money? 'Fine. How much do you need?'

He looks shocked. Obviously, he wasn't expecting me to be so easily convinced. Having Aaron in my office is not only a risk to my patients' safety and mental well-being, it also serves as a painful reminder of how little I have done to help my younger brother, and I don't feel like confronting this guilt.

I don't know how things started going so wrong for him. When he joined the forces, he was so full of enthusiasm and had a real lust for life. He was on track to do incredible things. He constantly impressed his superiors and won awards, and he was surrounded by friends who supported him.

Then, without warning, Dad received a call to say Aaron was being sent home and he should consider himself lucky they're not getting the police involved.

Aaron changed overnight. Gone was the vibrancy we loved; all that was left behind was a shell containing nothing but bitterness and anger.

It destroys me to look at him now. I should have done more to help him, but Aaron has always been evasive, and I just feel so powerless with him. I gave up hope without even giving him a chance.

'How much have you got?' he asks, shame coating his words.

I open the wallet I am still holding. 'Fifty. And some change,' I say. He looks to the ceiling and his shoulders drop. 'It isn't enough?'

'No, it's not that. I just ...'

I wait with one eyebrow raised, but he just shrugs. Starting to feel frustrated with Aaron's inability to speak his truth, I say, 'Come on. There's an ATM downstairs.' I just want him out of here.

We head down in silence, the space in the lift feeling much smaller than it really is. I want to reach my arms out to stop the walls from closing in.

It isn't until I'm tapping my pin into the ATM that Aaron speaks up again. 'Dad looked rough the other day,' he says conversationally.

I look up at him. Aaron is a fine one to talk. He looks like he hasn't slept in weeks and he could really do with a shave. He's not wrong about Dad, though. 'Yeah,' I say, yanking the money from the machine. 'Don't worry – I'll keep an eye on him.'

He grunts in acknowledgment and takes the notes from my hand. 'I'll pay you back,' he tells me, before nodding goodbye and stalking off down the road.

I watch him go, sadness overwhelming me.

CHAPTER 7

Georgia throws her arms around my legs, and I bend to return her embrace. She clings to me harder, and I scoop her up into my arms and kiss her forehead.

'Have a great day at school, sweetie,' I tell her, putting her back down so she can grab her bag and run out the door, eager to learn. She's an incredible human being and my pride in her is overwhelming.

'You going to be hanging around the house all morning?' Sarah asks me, jangling her keys in her hand.

'Yes. I've got no appointments this morning, so I thought I'd catch up on some paperwork at home.'

Sarah grunts, clearly not pleased with my presence in the home *I* pay for. 'Right, well, I've got some shopping to do. I'll be back by midday.'

I get the message loud and clear: she wants me out before she returns. We've reached the point where we can no longer be in the same building at the same time. Fine by me. I've got an appointment after lunch, anyway.

The second the door clicks shut behind them, I breathe a sigh of relief. As much as I love being around my daughter, there's something special about having the house to myself. It grants me a freedom that fills me with optimism.

I head into the kitchen and put the kettle on when the doorbell chimes, ruining my good mood.

Tutting, I head back into the hall and pull open the door. 'Dad?'

Dad is standing on my doorstep, a cigarette dangling from his lips. He takes the burning butt out of his mouth and stubs it against the brickwork. 'Alright, Zack?' Smiling at me, he lets himself in.

'Everything okay, Dad?' It isn't unusual for him to visit, but he always calls first in case I'm not here.

'I was just visiting a friend and thought I'd pop in, see how you are,' he says. His body looks particularly tense today, like he's done a round with Mike Tyson.

The kettle is bubbling wildly and pops to announce it's finished boiling. Dad leads the way into the kitchen. His posture is hunched, making him look inches shorter than he is.

I set to making him a cup of tea. 'Have you spoken to Aaron?' I'm nervous to ask in case he knows I lent Aaron the money Dad refused to give him.

'No. I think your mum has,' he says with a scowl.

'How is he? Do you know?' I ask, nervous to hear the answer. If Aaron admitted to Dad that I gave him the money, I know I'll be in Dad's bad books. I hate upsetting Dad when he's always there for me. At least one of his sons should be good to him.

I have always had a good relationship with Dad, built on respect and honesty, whereas my father's relationship with Aaron is the complete opposite. It's strained and painful to witness. As a boy, I'd often see Dad staring at Aaron with a knowing look in his eye. It was like he could see something no one else could, and that has only persisted into Aaron's adulthood.

'God knows. I didn't ask. But you know how he is – trouble.'

'What's he up to, do you think?'

Dad scoffs. 'Trust me, I don't want to know. I know stuff about that boy that'll make your hair curl.'

I wish I knew what Dad knows about Aaron that makes him so wound up, but I know if I ask, he'll just brush me off and it'll create a tense atmosphere between us and I don't want that. There are enough bad vibes in this house as it is.

He takes a sip of his drink and coughs into the mug, spraying brown liquid everywhere.

'Jesus, Dad. Go and sit down.' Dad goes to take a seat in the living room, still coughing, whilst I wipe up the splattered tea.

When I enter the room, he's wincing and rubbing his neck. 'Dad, are you okay?' It's a loaded question. Dad hates being seen as weak, and sickness is high on his list of weaknesses.

'I'm fine, lad. I've just got a little sniffle, that's all.'

But he's deathly white and I can't resist pushing it. 'Even so, I think you should see a doctor.'

He waves me away. 'Oh, shush. You sound just like your mum. Whining, all the damn time.'

I recoil in shock. Dad very rarely reprimands me, let alone speaks badly about Mum. Maybe Dad is feeling far worse than he lets on. I know he means no harm by it. It's a long-running joke that Dad is a stubborn old fart when it comes to seeing a doctor. I reckon it's because he hates to look weak, but Mum says he's just a lazy git. She says it with love, of course.

Now, I need to work this carefully. Trying to convince him to seek help from a doctor will only make the old bastard dig his heels in even further. 'Sorry, Dad. We just care about you.'

He laughs this time, seeing right through me. 'And don't give me your guilt-trip crap, either. I'm fine.'

The line is drawn. Conversation over.

He sets his mug down on the coffee table, ignoring the coaster. I bristle and fight the urge to move the cup to prevent a stain. 'How's work?' he asks, his usual check-in.

I frown, but knowing I'll get nowhere by trying to push the subject matter, I give up and change the subject. 'Oh, same as always. Tough, but rewarding, you know?' I avert my gaze. I can feel his eyes boring into me, digging their way into my secrets. Heat rushes through me and I pull at the neck of my shirt in an attempt to cool off.

Lo and behold, he asks the one question I prayed he'd keep to himself. 'Any more *problematic* clients?'

I shake my head far too quickly. 'No. It's all good.'

He doesn't believe me. He can see the lie written all over my face. I grab his mug and take it into the kitchen to escape his stare, but he follows me.

His tone is hard, and I wince in anticipation of his next words. 'Zack, you know you have to behave yourself, don't you? You promised to put more effort into your marriage and leave work where it belongs – at the office.'

I wince again. I know what I promised, but if he were to meet Millie, he'd understand. He'd like her.

Besides, nothing is going on, I try to convince myself. Nothing for *her*, anyway. My side of the story may be a little different. I'm well aware that the roots of obsession are digging deep, but it's not like I'm going to act on it.

Just because I saved her number in my personal phone doesn't mean anything is going to happen. It was just a precaution. A way to check in on her safety.

I shake my head. My relationship with Millie is purely professional. 'You've got nothing to worry about, Dad. You can trust me.'

He looks far from satisfied, but I'm relieved to see him nodding.

CHAPTER 8

.

I arrive at work earlier than usual, driven by a curious desire to make my desk immaculate. It's a ridiculous notion, really, to think that Millie would even notice the state of my workspace.

Nevertheless, I meticulously arrange every sheet of paper, pen, and piece of IT equipment, ensuring they are perpendicular and perfectly aligned. By the time she saunters in, a coy smile playing on her lips, my desk is a picture of orderly perfection.

It's just a shame my thoughts don't match my environment.

As Millie greets me, I catch her eyes lingering on my crisp white shirt that I wear most days. I like how it accentuates my tanned skin, and I've also rolled up the sleeves to show off my muscular arms. A pathetic action, but I can't fight the urge to impress this woman.

After speaking to Dad about Millie, I have not been able to stop thinking about her. She's more than a client – she's forbidden fruit, and it's killing me that I can't take a bite. My lack of professionalism scares the hell out of me, but I can't help these thoughts. Something deep inside me knows she's different. She just feels *worth it*. What is it about Millie O'Neale that captivates me?

We take our seats opposite each other and a wave of giddiness washes over me, reminiscent of a schoolboy's excitement before his first dance. My heart flutters, and I find myself struggling to maintain my composure in her presence.

Millie lowers herself back into her chair, her movements measured and cautious. She looks so much more relaxed in my presence now. I think now that our first session is out of the way, she can ease into her appointment a little more smoothly.

'How are you today?' I ask, my voice gentle.

Her lips curve into a smile that reveals her pristine, pearly whites. Despite the brightness of her grin, there's a lingering sadness written on her features. A stray tendril of hair escapes from behind her ear and she lets it hang there. I resist the urge to reach out and stroke it.

'I'm okay,' she replies, but her words sound heavy.

I study her carefully, analysing her fragility. Despite her assurances, it's clear she's far from okay. There's an edginess to her demeanour made more prominent by her wringing hands. 'How are things at home?'

Silence descends on us as Millie's gaze drifts out the window, her eyes taking in the bustling scene outside. Through the glass, we watch people hurry past, all engrossed in their own life. Their own dramas. The hubbub of outside contrasts with the quiet in the room, making me feel peaceful despite the intensity of our conversation.

Millie cuts through the calm. 'It's …' She closes her eyes. 'I'm getting by.'

I lean forward, pressing my chest against my clipboard. '*Getting by* isn't the goal, though, is it? Don't you think you deserve to be happy? What does "happy" look like to you?'

She blushes, but doesn't say anything, reverting to looking out the window. She shakes her head, the movement barely perceptible.

'I think you deserve the world,' I blurt out, the words escaping my lips before I can stop them. The moment they're spoken, I feel a rush of embarrassment, and my mouth snaps shut.

But, she just smiles – a genuine, warm smile. She's beyond beautiful. 'Who am I to argue with a professional?' Her tone is shy, yet playful, and I can't help but grin.

It's time I redirect the course of our conversation from Millie to her boyfriend, Dexter. 'Tell me about him. Dexter.' I've already seen the bruising the bastard leaves on her, but as a person he's a total stranger, and I need to know what I'm dealing with here.

'We've been together forever. Over four years.' She swallows hard. 'On and off.' My eyes are drawn to the delicate bobbing of her throat. 'We met on a night out in Liverpool. He lived up there at the time and was a real *jack-the-lad*, you know? Things started off so good. He was sweet and attentive.' She glances away.

'What changed?'

Her shoulders lift in a half-hearted shrug. She looks emotionally exhausted. 'His sister died and everything just ... shifted. He couldn't cope, and the only way he could handle that was to get mad.'

'When did his sister die?'

'Over a year ago.'

I lean back in my chair, lips pressed together. This beautiful woman has been beaten for over twelve months. I feel my blood pressure rise. I think about my wife. Sat at home, provided for, safe. It makes me mad to think about how ungrateful Sarah is when women like Millie don't even have a hint of the kindness they deserve. I force my attention back to Millie.

She blurts out. 'But he doesn't hurt me often. Maybe once a fortnight?'

'Millie ... It sounds to me like his sister's death was just a poor excuse to start abusing you. But what's his excuse for continuing?' It comes out before I even realise it's happening. I hate to throw around accusations, preferring to hone in on my client and their personal needs. But Dexter sounds like such an arsehole. And I need Millie to realise that. I can't have her making excuses for this man.

Her eyes grow wide, a flicker of realisation dawns. This moment marks the first crucial step in empowering her by nurturing that seed of doubt already planted in her mind. Now that Millie's trust in me has grown, I want to give her the courage she needs to break free from this toxic cycle she's trapped in. And sometimes, the truth needs to be presented loudly and clearly.

Tears spill over her cheeks, and I head over to my desk to grab a box of tissues. She takes one and dabs her face. She looks even more stunning when she cries. Her blue eyes glisten and her cheeks pinken. She looks like an innocent doll. 'He hides behind this *nice man* façade. It's really confusing.'

When her sobs ease, I reassure her. 'I know this is hard, but it doesn't have to be like this. You can have the happiness you deserve, Millie.'

She looks doubtful and returns to looking out the window. A tiny hiccup escapes her. I can see she's starting to shut down, so I shift the focus of our conversation to keep her talking. 'What do you like doing? What makes you happy?' I ask.

This time, her smile is genuine, radiating a warmth that spreads through me. 'I go to the gym most evenings,' she says, a hint of enthusiasm creeping into her voice between the hiccups. 'I find working out a great escape. It's *me* time. You know?'

I beam at her. 'That's great news, Millie. Looking after yourself is good for your mind.'

We spend the rest of the session in general chit-chat, getting to know each other better. It feels so natural, and it comes as a shock when Chelsea knocks on the door. 'Sorry to interrupt. It's just that your next patient has been waiting for ten minutes. I did knock before, but you told me to wait.'

Millie immediately jumps up. 'Oh, gosh! I'm so sorry to have kept you.' She reaches for my hand, and I shake it lightly.

Electricity pulses through my fingers. She looks into my eyes and bites her bottom lip. I feel a shift in the universe that sends a shiver down my spine. And a twinge in my groin.

Chapter 9

Cursing, I pull into a parking space the farthest away from the supermarket door. The car park is full. Why does everyone need to panic-buy ten minutes before the supermarket shuts on a Sunday? I only need a loaf of bread and a bag of coffee for the office, and now I'm faced with an unpleasant walk in the rain.

Tutting, I get out of the car and jog over to the covered path to avoid the rain. I walk past the gym, cringing at the music blasting through the open doors. Don't get me wrong, I'm in good shape, but I much prefer the solitude and fresh air of a run. The thought of getting sweaty in a room full of pumped-up people feels somewhat vulgar.

But then, I spy the one person with whom I wouldn't mind spending time in a sweat-clouded gym. She walks towards me with her head down, oblivious to her surroundings.

Millie.

Seeing Millie out of context has caught me off guard and I don't know the best way to react, so I act like a silly teenager. I hide behind a couple walking hand in hand so that she doesn't see me. I take a deep breath to pull myself together, then step away from the couple who have now stopped to kiss passionately in the rain.

Millie has walked straight past me and is heading into the gym. She has a huge bag hooked over her shoulder and she's wearing the tightest, tiniest shorts, revealing incredibly muscular, tanned thighs. I swallow down the pool of spit forming in my mouth. I don't want to dribble.

I watch as she scans in with her membership card at the front desk and walks through into the crowd. And then she's gone.

Disappointment crushes me. I didn't even get a good look at her face, and I'm left with a burning desire to look her in the eyes and talk to her. I want to check that she's okay.

I continue my walk to the supermarket in glum silence. My feet drag and my heart feels heavy.

'Dr Briens?' A familiar voice calls over to me as I walk through the doors and head for the bakery section. 'Long time no see!'

I turn to find the wrinkly features of Mrs Rogan, a retired school teacher who was once so badly beaten by her drug addict son, she was too afraid to leave her house.

'Mrs Rogan! How are you?' I greet her warmly with my friendliest smile, though truth be told, I'm not in the mood to chat right now. Once Mrs Rogan starts talking, she is very hard to stop.

'I couldn't be better. And that's all down to you.'

My stiff back relaxes. Mrs Rogan was a difficult case. Her love for her son was so strong that she found accepting his criminal behaviour and disgusting treatment of her hard to bear. Not only was he hurting her for money, he blamed her for his misdemeanours.

'I'm so glad to hear you're doing well. You did such an excellent job with your recovery.'

'Dr Briens, I feel like I never thanked you properly. It's down to you that I found the courage to start being myself again and once that clicked into place, I was able to help my son.'

'Yeah? Oh, that's incredible to hear!'

'He's at university now. Studying criminology.'

I couldn't be happier. I do love a happier ending.

As Mrs Rogan natters on about how proud she is of the son who put her in hospital, my mind drifts to Millie. I wish I would apply the same professionalism to her as I did with Mrs Rogan, but Millie is alluring beyond measure. She does things to me that make me feel incredibly uncomfortable and yet exhilarated in equal measure. I curse my lack of control over my thoughts and vow to never extend that to my behaviour.

Mrs Rogan finishes her monologue with a hug and wanders off to the tinned goods aisle.

I end up getting more than I intended to buy, to give myself some more thinking time.

When I walk back towards my car, the gym is so loud and there's no sign of Millie anywhere, but I step inside to shelter from the rain. And maybe to get a closer look.

'Can I help you?' A young girl with a huge smile and bright features calls over to me from the front desk.

'Oh – no, thank you. I was just being nosy.'

She screws her face up at me, clearly unhappy with a soggy guy craning his neck to see through to the dance studios. 'This gym is for members only,' she tells me, folding her arms. 'No walk-ins.'

I'd better go. I don't fancy taking on a five-foot woman with huge biceps. I give her a curt nod and turn away.

'Dr Briens?' Her voice rings out, sweet and musical.

My heart skips a beat as I turn around to face her. Her blonde curls are escaping her hair tie. Tendrils have gathered around her face, sticking to the sweat slicked across her forehead. Yet, she smiles without a hint of embarrassment over her dishevelled appearance. A truly sexy personality trait.

'Hi!' I say back, uncertainly. She walks towards me, dabbing her face with a small towel. She brings the towel away and I can't fail to notice a bruise under her left eye. I can't breathe. I long to reach out and touch it; I want to stroke away the pain. Instead, I just bite my teeth together, forcing back the words I want to say. I force myself back into my professional mannerisms with a shake of my shoulders.

'What are you doing here?' she asks, standing uncomfortably close, but I can't bring myself to step away. Her scent is alluring.

'Oh, I was just enquiring about a membership.' I cast a glance at the girl behind the desk, who is watching me with amusement. I need to get out of here before I make a fool of myself. I am sopping wet and clutching a bag of groceries. It doesn't take a genius to figure out I'm lying.

So, I'm surprised when Millie asks me, 'Do you want to grab a coffee or something?' She looks at her watch. 'I have a bit of time before I need to be home.'

My initial response is to refuse. I feel like I'm crossing the patient boundary lines I have always held so close to my heart. 'Sure,' I say, cursing my weakness.

She leads me to a coffee shop around the corner where the baristas look less than pleased to be working on a wet Sunday evening. We take a seat at a booth in the corner and sit in awkward silence. I drum my fingers on the table.

'So, what were you really doing at the gym?' she asks, smiling over her cappuccino.

'I told you, just enquiring about a membership.'

She giggles quietly. 'You're a terrible liar, Dr Briens.'

As embarrassed as I feel, I can't help but smile at her bashful cheekiness. 'Fine. You got me. I saw you go in and I wanted to check if you're okay.' I gesture at the bruising beneath her eye. 'And please, call me Zack.'

She touches her face like she's just remembered the bruise. Is the violence so frequent that she no longer realises she's injured? 'It's nothing,' she mumbles, placing her cup carefully on the table and wrapping her fingers around the mug.

'It doesn't look like nothing,' I press.

She scowls at me. 'I didn't realise this would be another therapy session ... Zack.'

She's right, of course. I have ambushed her outside the only place she probably feels is hers. I'm such an idiot.

The silence returns with a cloud of tension. It engulfs us and I wish I hadn't come here. I should have left my relationship with Millie in the office. This is far too informal, too intimate, and I don't know how to handle it.

She sighs. 'I appreciate you caring about me. I feel like you're the only person who does.'

And with those devastating words, all of my stress disappears. 'What about your family? Where are they?'

She shrugs. 'Gone. Mum and Dad moved to Spain just days after I turned eighteen, and we haven't really bothered to keep in touch. It feels like too much effort. And I have no brothers or sisters, so ...'

She's alone. Or, she was. She isn't anymore.

'Do you have anyone else to talk to about ... you know?'

She smiles sadly. 'About Dexter? No, only you.'

Despite myself, I feel my chest swell with pride. 'Well, I'll always be here for you,' I admit. My sympathy runs too deep to hold it back anymore. 'I want to help you.'

She puffs out a chuckle. 'Yeah ... because you're paid to.'

'I'm here right now, aren't I?'

She squints at me, biting her full bottom lip. She's sussing me out and I don't blame her. With what's happening at home, I can understand why she struggles to trust the men in her life.

As if whipped out of a trance, Millie gasps and looks at her watch. 'Shit, I've got to go!' She stands and turns to leave, but changes her mind and turns back to me. 'Thank you, Zack.' And then, she bends to plant a kiss on my cheek.

I watch her go, my fingers pressed to my cheek where she has just placed her sweet lips on my skin.

There's something special about Millie O'Neale, and I'm falling for her.

Hook, line, and sinker.

Shit.

CHAPTER 10

Trying to mask my sense of urgency, I tuck Georgia into bed, moving swiftly through the routine. I read her *The Gruffalo*, give her a hug goodnight, and press a long kiss to her forehead. Then I run downstairs to slip on my shoes.

'Where are you going?' Sarah's voice cuts through my thoughts as she emerges from the kitchen, glass of wine in hand, filled to the brim.

'Out,' I reply curtly, shrugging on my coat with a sense of determination. 'Don't get so drunk that you can't look after Georgia,' I say, casting her an accusatory glance.

She scoffs in response. 'It's *one* glass, Zack. At least I'm here for her. Unlike someone I know ...' She turns her back on me and disappears into the living room, the door closing behind her with a definitive thud.

What she doesn't know is that I have asked Mum to pay them a visit in an hour. Just in case.

For a moment, I contemplate the disconnect between Sarah and I, the gap that seems to grow wider with each passing day. But as quickly as the thought surfaces, I push it aside. Whatever issues we may have, they pale in comparison to the magnetic pull that draws me out tonight. I've got better things to do than argue with my wife.

Since my impromptu meeting with Millie in the coffee shop, I have spent every second thinking about her. My obsession is growing into something unbearable. It's like an itch I can't scratch and it's driving me insane.

As I drive to the other side of town, I contemplate my actions. I know I am crossing so many professional boundaries, but surely if no one else knows, then it doesn't matter. Besides, it's my job to help Millie, and the more information I have, the better job I can do.

I pull up against the kerb and take it all in. Her house is pleasant. Smaller than mine, but I imagine her estate agent boyfriend earns a fraction of what I make. But still, the detached house is tidy and welcoming to look at.

Evergreen trees surround the property, providing a shield from prying eyes, so I step out of the car and inch my way closer. I have to step into the bushes to get a good look. The closest neighbour's house must be over a hundred yards away, but I still feel the sickening thrill of potentially getting caught.

There are no cars in Millie's drive, and the lights are off, so I assume the house is empty. The magnetism I feel towards Millie grows stronger with each second I spend outside her home.

Headlights appear around the corner, and I press deeper into the bush. A black Mercedes pulls into the drive, and I gasp when Millie climbs out of the driver's seat, pulling her gym bag out with her.

She strides into her house, no doubt feeling more secure with Dexter not at home. As she goes to close the door, she pauses, staring straight at me. I sink back, deeper amongst the leaves, burying myself in the darkness. I hold my breath, even though I know there's no way she can see me in the dark. Seconds that feel like hours pass before the light emanating from Millie's hallway fades as she closes the front door behind her.

I finally allow myself to breathe again. My heart is pounding in my chest, and I feel sick. That was far too close for comfort.

I sit and wait for my nerves to stop tingling and I laugh under my breath. This is ludicrous. What power does Millie have over me that makes me behave like this? I must be going insane.

Despite doubting my sanity, seeing Millie again has fed my fire. Screw professionalism and boundaries. My resolve to keep my distance melts away and a tension that was squeezing every single one of my muscles lets go.

Millie's is an exceptional case, that I now know requires an exceptional course of action. I just need to figure out what that action looks like.

With one last glance at the house, I go to leave, but a sudden light inside makes me hesitate. The light is coming from upstairs – her bedroom.

I shift left to get a better view. Millie's silhouette appears by the window, and she steps closer, her petite and firm body coming into focus. She takes my breath away.

I watch as she pulls off her T-shirt, revealing a black sports bra. My mouth drops open when she reaches back to undo the clasp. My pulse hammers in my neck and try as I might, I'm unable to take my eyes off her.

She pauses momentarily as she looks down the road, probably waiting for Dexter's arrival. She frowns, and I can feel her nerves from here. My heart goes out to her. How can men be so cruel? Millie shouldn't be living in fear like this.

I watch as she loosens her bra and shakes it off with a wiggle of her shoulders. I groan into my fist, unable to contain my excitement.

Her nipples are round and pink, her breasts firm and inviting.

My heart is racing.

'Oh, Millie. What are you doing to me?' I moan.

The pressure in my underwear is agony. I slowly unzip my fly and allow my penis out. My hand clasps my erection, and I start to pump.

It doesn't take long until I am on the verge of losing myself. A tension works its way up from my lower abdomen to my neck. My spare hand clutches the tree trunk in front of me and my knees threaten to buckle. My eyes squeeze shut as a shudder runs down the length of my entire body and semen spurts onto the ground.

Then, a voice calls out behind me. 'What the fuck do you think you're doing?'

CHAPTER 11

Dread pounds in my throat as I run back to my car, pressing my manhood back into my pants. I slam the door behind me, wrench the car into gear and slam my foot on the accelerator, tearing away from the kerb.

In the rearview mirror, I catch a fleeting glimpse of eyes aflame with disgust, but I'm moving too fast to make out a face. There's a dog sitting by the guy's feet, its squished face also seeming horrified. Blood rushes to my cheeks, burning with shame. No one should see *that* when out walking their dog.

'Shit, shit, shit,' I mutter under my breath, my hands sweating as I grip the steering wheel. How could I have been so utterly stupid? I let myself get carried away. I lost control of my senses.

Fuck! I'm such a fool.

I fight through the shame as the distance between me and my shocking behaviour grows in my mind. Maybe whoever spotted me didn't see me clearly. Maybe they didn't actually see what I was doing. After all, it was dark and he was on the other side of the road.

I breathe deeply, in through my nose, out through my mouth. Yes, that's it. He couldn't have seen me properly. I quash my paranoia and eventually my thoughts drift back to Millie.

I want to show her the life she could be living. A life with me. I imagine picking her up, throwing her over my shoulder, and taking her to bed. *My* bed. Arousal tickles my groin once again and I shake my head to remove the image of her breasts from my brain.

To wake up beside her would be a dream come true. Keeping her safe and happy. Watching her become a mother to Georgia.

I laugh at my silly fantasy. It's never going to happen.

Then thoughts of what just happened come flooding back. It's like a tug of war. Every time I manage to divert my attention, the memory fights its way to the foreground of my mind.

I groan with the confusion of it all.

The streetlights zoom past in a blur as I navigate the twists and turns of the road, ignoring the speed limit in a poor attempt to outrun my own thoughts.

Being a weeknight, the High Street is quiet. A young couple floats out of a restaurant arm in arm, laughing at some joke, the woman stroking her partner's arm affectionately. A group of teenagers lurk in the doorway of a closed charity shop, looking like they're up to no good with their hoods pulled high and heads dipped low.

As I pass the Rose and Crown, a pub notorious for brawls and drug deals, I spot Aaron treading down the steps, hands stuffed into his pockets. He's deep in conversation with a man beside him.

I'm stunned. I always thought Aaron was a loner, so to see him with a friend feels jarring. What's more surprising is how well put-together Aaron's friend is. He's a far cry from my brother's usually dishevelled appearance.

They head down the road in front of my car and I slow to a snail's pace, drawn in by curiosity. They're laughing together, Aaron completely at ease in this man's company. The friend is taller than Aaron's six-foot-four-inch frame. He doesn't have Aaron's broad shoulders though; he's gangly and lithe, clumsy-looking. But he's a good-looking man. Someone I can imagine Millie being with.

If she wasn't destined to be with me.

I decide I've wasted enough time looking at my brother and drive away, forgetting all about the strange friendship.

***

As the familiar streets of my neighbourhood come into view, a sense of dread settles over me. This house, my marriage, feels like a cage and I resent it with a passion. I need to break free from it just as much as Millie does from hers.

I pull into my drive, the engine falling silent as I sit there, gripping the steering wheel like it's my life ring. The thought of stepping through that door, of facing the reality of my life and the woman in it, fills me with a heavy sense of despair.

I finally convince myself to enter the house. As I step over the threshold, the sound of Georgia crying immediately hits me. I take the stairs two at a time, Georgia's sobs pulling at my core. She sounds so sad, so desperate. I round the corner to find her sitting on the bathroom floor, in the dark. The smell of vomit is noxious, knocking me backwards. I fight the urge to cover my nose.

'Baby?' I switch on the light. My heart breaks when I see my precious little girl curled up on the cold floor tiles, her clammy head resting on the toilet seat. Green foamy vomit is pooled in the toilet water in thick globs.

'Daddy?' Her voice is weak. She tries to lift her head to look at me, but it slips back down, her eyes flickering open.

In an instant, I am by her side. I loop one arm around her tiny frame, and with my free hand I scrape back her hair from her sweat-dampened face. 'What's happened, sweetheart?'

'I was sick,' she says, stating the obvious. 'I feel poorly, Daddy.'

'Where's your mother?' I try to keep the fury out of my voice. How can a mother leave her child in this state? Does she even realise what's happening? I imagine her passed out in a drunken stupor downstairs and I grind my teeth together.

Georgia shrugs weakly. I reach over and flush the toilet to let Georgia's dinner swirl down into the U-bend. The stench still lingers.

'Are you ready to get into bed?'

Georgia nods. 'I think so, Daddy.' She attempts to smile. She looks so vulnerable, so sweet. I wish I could wrap my arms around her for the next – well, forever – and protect her from all the bad in the world.

With gentle hands, I scoop her up and cradle her to my chest. I carry her into her bedroom and carefully lay her down on the bed, smoothing the covers over her. As soon as her head hits the pillow, Georgia curls up and her eyes flutter closed. I stand there for a moment, watching her chest rise and fall with each heavy breath.

With a deep sigh, I tear myself away and head back into the bathroom to grab a clean washcloth and run it under the cool water. I return to my baby girl's bedroom and place the cloth on her forehead to cool her fever. She doesn't wake.

I sit in the armchair covered in soft toys and watch her for a few minutes. Horrifying thoughts of Georgia choking on her vomit swarm me, and I decide to sleep in here tonight, just in case.

Mind made up, I go to fetch the sick bowl from under the kitchen sink. As I head downstairs, I hear Sarah clattering around in the kitchen. I push the door open with such ferocity it slams into the cupboard behind, marking the wood.

Sarah is stacking glasses in the dishwasher like she doesn't have a care in the world.

'Where the fuck have you been?' My tone is harsh, the words firing from my tongue.

Her mouth gapes open, but I don't want to listen to her bullshit, so I carry on the onslaught. 'Georgia is up there spewing her guts up, scared, and desperate for a parent to take care of her! And what are *you* doing? Sitting on your fat arse drinking yourself stupid. You're a waste of fucking space!' Spit flies from my mouth. 'I don't know why I married you!'

She stares at me with absolute hate. Our marriage is dripping with poison. 'For your information,' she bites, '*I* have been taking care of Georgia whilst *you* were out doing God-knows-what!'

I flinch as I cast my mind back to where I was this evening; to what I was doing.

She jabs a fork in my direction and continues. 'If you think for one fucking second that I'm not there when our girl needs me, you're more stupid than you look.'

I bristle. My conscience is telling me she's right; maybe I should have been here, but that doesn't excuse Sarah's bullshit. 'Bollocks. She was all alone in the dark, Sarah.'

'For about five seconds! I changed her sheets, Zack. She couldn't sleep in that mess. I ran downstairs to put the washing machine on, and whilst I was doing that I heard you come home and go up to her, so I figured I could rush through a few jobs before I took the sick bowl upstairs.' She gestures at the pink bowl we have reserved specifically for tummy upsets.

I scowl at her, my anger refusing to dissipate. I don't like the sensation of guilt that niggles at my stomach. It's pissing me off.

'You know what I find hilarious?' she mutters as she steps closer. I can smell the wine on her breath. 'You're blaming me, but Zack, the only person who wasn't here for her, was *you*. You're a fucking hypocrite. Now, if you don't mind, I'm going back upstairs to be with our daughter.' She turns away, but stops before she leaves my view and turns back to me. She looks spent. '*Zack, we both know you're a good dad. But please stop painting me as the bad guy. We both know that's not true.'*

Sarah's accusation hangs in the air. With clenched hands, I watch as she turns on her heel and storms off, her back rigid with anger and each footstep echoing with condemnation.

She's right for once – I am a good dad. Georgia is the centre of my world. Tonight was a momentary glitch. A brief indulgence.

I make a promise to myself that I will be a better father to Georgia, and I know how to fulfil that promise. I need to remove Sarah from this house. She's the one pushing me away.

Is Sarah a good mum?

I grab the brandy from the cupboard and pour myself a sensible measure to take the edge off. Yes, Sarah is a good mum, I can't deny that. But that's what scares me. A good mum will win any battle in a divorce court.

My thoughts begin to spiral and I down my drink. No, this is all too much. I need to stay focused on what matters. And what matters right now is Georgia, and by extension, Millie – she's the answer to my prayers. She can complete my family and fill the hole in my life. She will help me convince a judge that Georgia is better off with me.

I can see it now. True happiness. Me, Georgia, and Millie on my arm.

A picture complete.

CHAPTER 12

With Georgia at a birthday party and Sarah at her Saturday morning bootcamp, I revel in the rare moment of solitude. I lose myself in the rhythmic pounding of my feet on the treadmill in the garage, the monotone sounds of the newsreader on TV a backdrop to my thoughts.

After I've worked up a sweat, I enjoy the hot spray of the shower, washing away the sweat and lingering tensions. My workout has left me feeling hungry, so I head to the kitchen to cook breakfast. I switch on the radio and do a little jig to the Beatles whilst I prepare my food.

As I settle down to a plate of fried eggs on toast, the ring of the doorbell shatters my peace. Irritation simmers beneath my skin as I make my way to the door, leaving my meal to go cold.

'Aaron!' I greet my brother with scorn. I love my brother, but he only ever comes around here when he wants something.

'You alright, bro?' he says, as he steps around me and walks straight into my home, the smell of aftershave wafting in after him. He's pushed his hair back and is wearing dark blue jeans with a leather jacket I haven't seen before. He looks good!

Relief washes over me. Maybe Aaron is sorting himself out. Maybe he's here to make amends. 'Come in!' I mutter, my voice soaked in sarcasm as I close the door behind him. 'I'm actually in the middle of something ...' But Aaron is gone, disappeared into my house. I find him in the dining room, tucking into my damn breakfast. 'What the fuck, Aaron?'

He glances up at me, a picture of nonchalance. 'Sorry. I haven't eaten. You can cook more though, right?'

My resentment towards my brother bubbles to the surface. Anger threatens to take over me as I swallow back the harsh language I long to use. Dad is right about him – he is an idiot. I sink into the chair on the other side of the table, crossing my legs. 'What do you want, Aaron?'

He takes his time, savouring every bite of my meal before deigning to answer. 'I thought I'd just come and see you.'

I scoff. 'You don't ever come just to visit. You want something.'

The clatter of cutlery against the plate punctuates his shrug. 'What can I say? You're wrong. I thought we should talk.'

'What about?'

He wipes my toast over the plate, soaking up every last drop of egg yolk. He's deep in thought like he's weighing up his next words, but my patience is wearing thin. He sighs deeply and I see sadness flit across his face, but I don't care enough to acknowledge it. 'It doesn't matter,' he says. 'This was a stupid idea. Can we just forget this happened?'

'Look, you're here now. What do you want to talk about?'

'I've changed my mind.'

I'm tantalisingly close to getting Aaron to open up. I can see he's on the cusp of a big revelation. 'No, don't clam up on me, Aaron. What's going on?'

He just groans and I curse myself for my lack of skill. Putting pressure on someone is the quickest way to prevent them from taking the plunge. But, lo and behold, Aaron pushes his shoulders back and stands taller. 'No, it's fine. He got it wrong.' A desperation lies behind his eyes that makes me wish things were different between us.

'Who got it wrong?'

He looks me in the eyes like he's imploring me to read beneath them. He wants me to know something he doesn't have the courage to say out loud. I frown at him, trying to decide whether I want to make the effort to probe further. No, it'll be a waste of time. I know from experience if I try to get Aaron to open up to me, he'll put a great big wall up between us, which will only add to the tension precariously holding our relationship together.

'You know you can talk to me, right? When you're ready,' I say, though I pick up my empty plate to put an end to this conversation. I'd love to help my brother, but I just don't know how. He's an enigma my therapy skills can't cut through.

'How's Sarah?' he asks.

'Why?'

He cocks his head to the side. 'She's my sister-in-law. Am I not allowed to ask how she is?' He grins at me, and I know he's only asking to wind me up. He knows I hate my wife and he knows how uncomfortable I feel about their friendship. It's like they're ganging up on me. And now he's just being a prick.

I clench my teeth together. 'Just go, Aaron. If you just came here to wind me up ...'

'No. Not at all. I just ...'

'Why did you visit? You could have just called, or even better, sent a text?'

The fleeting sadness returns, a glimpse of the broken man beneath the silliness. For a split second, I can see the ghosts of Aaron's mysterious past crawling beneath his skin. But the moment passes and he shakes it off, forcing a smile back on his face. 'I guess I just wanted to come and eat your food.' He laughs, but the sound is hollow and strained.

I watch him go, leaving my door wide open in his wake. He walks away up my drive, his shoulders hunched against the weight of his demons.

We're worlds apart, my brother and I. Forever destined to misunderstand each other.

***

Sarah texts to let me know she's picked Georgia up from the party and now they're off to buy new school shoes. A twinge of annoyance flares within me at the thought of missing out on time with my daughter, but it's quickly overshadowed by the relief of avoiding my wife's company.

I'm bored and restless. I have already collected my dry-cleaning and pored through my notes for upcoming appointments, and now I'm twiddling my fingers.

It's no use. I can't resist.

I pull up down the road from Millie's house. Her driveway is empty and there's no sign of life inside the home. I drum my fingers against the steering wheel, studying the house's façade. It looks so ordinary, so unassuming – a stark contrast to the brutal reality that lies inside.

Memories of our previous conversations flood my mind: Millie's hushed confessions; the pain in her eyes as she described her boyfriend's insidious control; the way he monitors her every move, dictates her appearance, refuses her pleas to see her friends. And the punishments, the consequences of her *disobedience*. The thought makes my blood boil and my fists clench with the desire to save her from this sick bastard.

Before I can think better of it, I am out of the car. I knock on the front door, just in case. If Dexter answers, I can just say I have the wrong address. But when no one answers, I'm sure the house is empty. I glance around to check for nosy neighbours before slipping down the side of the house and into their garden. The lawn is pristine and the decking that wraps around the side of the house is immaculate, not a single weed in sight.

There's a double-door around the back of the house and I press my face against the glass, cupping my hands around my eyes so I can see inside. The living room is painted cream and adorned with cream carpets and gold accents. It's beautiful, but devoid of any hints of personality or warmth. It's almost clinical in appearance.

A gentle push reveals the lock on the door is flimsy, an invitation too tempting to resist. With a gentle shove, it slides open. I slip inside, blood pounding in my ears. The house is silent, but I strain to listen for any signs of life. Nothing.

Creeping through the living room, I make my way toward the kitchen. Time is of the essence; I need to be quick before someone comes home. My fear urges me to leave – to run away from this madness – but my curiosity wins, and my feet keep stepping forward, deeper into Millie's home.

I enter the kitchen. I've always thought the kitchen is the soul of a house, so it's a great place to learn about the people who live here. In this room, I catch a glimpse of the suffocating control that Millie has to endure. Bare, flawless countertops – not a single item or crumb sits on the work surfaces. The surfaces themselves sparkle and I can imagine Millie scrubbing away to ensure they meet Dexter's high standards. They're a testament to his need for dominance.

The rest of downstairs is equally lifeless, a façade of perfection masking the ugliness of their relationship. With a final glance at the empty driveway, I ascend the stairs, drawn to the main bedroom.

The master bedroom is dominated by an immaculately made king-sized bed. But, it's the dresser that catches my eye. A treasure trove longing to be explored.

Sudden voices outside make me freeze in my tracks. I hold my breath, inching towards the window. I spy two women strolling past, wearing lycra and pushing prams. They're deep in conversation and gesticulating wildly with their free hands. My heart races, adrenaline coursing through my veins. I need to hurry.

I force myself to breathe again. With trembling hands, I slide open the top dresser drawer. Jackpot. Lacy lingerie, meticulously arranged in tiny squares. Thongs and bras. Stockings and suspender belts. A tantalising glimpse into Millie's hidden world.

I pluck a delicate black thong from the drawer, bringing it to my lips. Inhaling deeply, I search for her scent, craving that intimate connection. Only the cloying fragrance of laundry detergent fills my nostrils. I pocket the thong.

I go to leave, but something else catches my eye as I pass the bathroom. I step inside to get a closer look. A splatter of red, stark against the white porcelain sink, and droplets scattered on the mirror. A macabre work of art. My blood runs cold, my mind reeling. This can't be happening.

I don't get time to panic as the sound of the front door slamming cuts through the silence.

CHAPTER 13

Paralysed by panic, I stand motionless. My breathing is shallow and ragged. I hear footsteps echo through the house as the person downstairs moves into the kitchen. A deep cough reverberates up the stairs, the sound deep and abrasive against my nerves. It's him – *Dexter*. I glance at the bathroom sink once more, the crimson blood stain evidence of what this man is capable of. A glacial chill runs through me. I need to get out of here. *Now*.

Dexter clatters around in the kitchen, slamming cupboard doors with such force the shower screen rattles next to me. I tread carefully over to the top of the stairs and peer over the railing. I strain to catch a glimpse of the kitchen, my heart pounding in my throat. I can't see far enough, so I take a few tentative steps down the stairs. He coughs again, then grunts as if he's in pain. He sounds like a troll.

With each careful step, I edge closer to the ground floor. I can finally peep around the corner, and I sigh with relief when I see the kitchen door is closed. Thank Christ. Seizing the opportunity, I lunge for the front door, my fingers scrabbling on the latch. I yank the door open and burst into the open air, my legs propelling me forward with a burst of adrenaline.

Hugging the front of the house, I keep low to avoid Dexter spotting me from the kitchen window. I inch along the front of the house until I reach the periphery. My stomach is in my mouth the entire time. I squeeze past the perfectly manicured hedge, its branches snagging my shirt and clawing at my skin as if trying to hold me back. I break free from the hedge's clutches and emerge on the pavement, my feet slamming onto the concrete.

My car is just metres away, glinting in the sunlight and I make a mad dash for it. The door handle feels cool and solid beneath my sweat-slicked palm. I launch myself inside and slam the door shut. Fumbling for the right key, my trembling hands desperately seek the ignition. Finally, the engine roars into life and I peel away from the kerb.

I scan the rear-view mirror and watch Millie's house recede into the distance. I can breathe again. I shift in my seat, the lump in my back pocket a reminder of my trophy. I pull out the tiny piece of black lace and hang it over the steering wheel. The close call was worth it.

But, I know what I've just witnessed will haunt me forever. The image of the blood-splattered sink – the evidence of Dexter's brutality – is seared into my mind. I am terrified for Millie.

I tap the screen on my dashboard, searching for Millie's number I have saved in my phone. As the distance widens between myself and Millie's abuser, the streets lined with houses gradually give way to huge oak trees. Their mighty height leans over my car, blocking my view of the countryside that surrounds me. I don't know where I am going, I just know I need to keep driving.

Millie's voice, soft and endearing, filters through the car speakers. 'Hello?'

'Hello, Millie. It's Zack.' I clear my throat. 'Dr Briens.'

She's stunned into silence. There's a hubbub of voices behind her. Eventually, she spits out, 'Oh! Hi, Zack. Everything okay?'

I find myself at a loss for words. Despite the apparent normalcy in Millie's tone, a nagging worry persists. Asking her directly feels pointless; she's hardly likely to admit whatever her boyfriend has subjected her to over the phone. Especially if she's in public.

Clearing my throat, I push ahead. 'Yeah, everything's fine. It's just that I had a cancellation this afternoon, and I was wondering if you'd like to come in for a session? No charge due to the short notice.' I don't mention that I am usually closed for appointments on Saturdays.

A brief silence hangs in the air before Millie responds. 'Oh, I don't know. I'm doing the shopping and if I don't head straight home, then ...' Her voice trails off, leaving the consequences unspoken.

My grip on the steering wheel tightens, making my knuckles ache. Grasping at a solution, I suggest, 'Can't you tell Dexter there's a new class you want to try at the gym?' When we went for a coffee, Millie confessed that Dexter has very high expectations of Millie's physique. The gym feels like a good excuse to escape him for the afternoon. She didn't go into detail, but I know from previous clients what can happen to a victim who dares gain a pound or two.

I hate asking her to lie like this. I know I am stepping way out of line here, but what choice do I have? How can I be sure Millie isn't seriously hurt without seeing her face to face?

The pause on the line is agonising, but relief washes over me when Millie agrees. 'Yeah, okay,' she says. 'I'll be there ASAP.'

CHAPTER 14

My phone rings when I'm en route to my office. The shrill ring makes me jump and I curse under my breath as I answer the call.

Sarah's pissed-off voice sounds through the car speakers, making my heart drop. 'Can you come and get Georgia? She's bored.'

Bored? She's been to a birthday party and shoe shopping already today. I highly doubt she's bored. Sarah's probably just fed up with looking after her and wants a drink.

'I can't right now. I have an emergency at work.'

Sarah tuts like my profession is an inconvenience. 'Can Georgia sit in the waiting room? I'll give her some pens and paper to bring along to keep her occupied.'

I pause, seething. How can I tell her to *fuck off* without igniting a huge argument for which I don't have the energy? Of course I want to see Georgia, but having her sit alone in my waiting room is hardly bonding time.

Sarah bleats on. 'Oh, come on, Zack! She misses you. You're never around anymore.'

I slam my fist into the dashboard, frustrated that I've allowed Sarah to get to me, and upset that I'm angry at the prospect of spending time with Georgia. Damn Sarah. And damn me for letting her get under my skin. 'Fine. I'll swing by in five minutes. Have her ready to leave when I pull up.'

Having fetched a grumpy and tired Georgia, I rush to the office, a man on a mission. With a flurry of activity, I turn on all the lights and crank up the heat, praying I can convince Millie this is a normal day at work and not a way to check she's okay after breaking into her home and witnessing evidence of a brutal beating.

Georgia kneels on the floor in front of the coffee table and settles down, clutching her crayons close to her chest, and immediately gets to work drawing. I look at her with fondness. She's such a good kid.

'Daddy needs to work now, okay? Make sure you wait in here. I won't be long.'

She nods, keeping her eyes on the swirls she's drawing.

The next twelve minutes feel like an eternity. My anxiety mounts with each tick of the clock. By the time Millie steps out of the lift, I'm wound tight. The sight of her floods me with an overwhelming sense of relief and the tension drains from my body. She's okay.

'Hey doc,' she greets me, her nose wrinkling at my intensity. But even as I smile at her, my eyes are scanning her, searching for any signs of harm. 'Cute kid,' she tells me, nodding at my daughter.

I'm relieved to see that her face is free of cuts or bruises, but there is no knowing what lies underneath her loose-fitting dress. From what I've seen since meeting Millie, I didn't think Dexter was particularly bothered about hiding the evidence of his temper. But maybe now he's seen sense. I could cry for her.

'Come in! Make yourself comfortable,' I tell her.

We step inside my office, and Millie scans the room with a wrinkled brow. 'It feels weird in here. No receptionist today?' Her question hangs in the air, a hint of curiosity tinged with something else. Uncertainty, perhaps, or a flicker of unease?

I force a smile and aim for a reassuring tone. 'It's her day off. So, today you have the pleasure of my undivided attention.'

'Oh, that's such a shame. I like her.'

I chuckle. Everyone loves Chelsea, and I can't fault her efficiency and competence. I should thank her more.

Millie heads over to the sofa and sits down slowly in her usual spot. I watch her carefully. She grimaces as her backside presses into the cushions. 'So, how come you wanted to see me today? You sounded pretty urgent on the phone.'

I click the door shut and sit down opposite her, not bothering with my notebook and pen. 'I wanted to check in on you. To make sure you're all right. I made a promise to look out for you, and I intend to keep it.' The words flow from my lips, a declaration of concern and support. But beneath the surface, a deeper, unspoken truth lurks – a promise I've made to myself to protect her.

Millie's gaze drops to the floor. 'I'm okay,' she murmurs, the words barely audible.

But I can see the cracks in her armour. Ignoring my internal voice that screams at me to remain professional, I press on with gentle firmness. 'No, Millie. You know you can be honest with me. This is a safe place.'

Tears slip down her cheeks. Going against my better judgement, I inch forward so our knees are touching. Her vulnerability erupts my sympathy. She edges even closer to me, only slightly, maybe an inch. It emboldens me to take her hand. To my delight, she doesn't pull away.

It's as if she's enjoying a gentle human touch after a year of nothing but violence.

I let her cry, handing her tissues. Eventually she speaks. 'I'm just so *tired*, Zack.'

'Tired?'

'I'm exhausted, constantly walking on eggshells, second-guessing my every move. No matter how hard I try, it's never enough.' She pauses, her gaze distant as if lost in a bittersweet memory. 'I miss the old Dexter. He was so attentive, so loving. We laughed until our sides hurt. We just ... connected ... you know?'

Oh, I know. I know very well. The connection between Millie and I is palpable. She'll realise it soon enough and she'll know there has never been anything between her and Dexter.

'His sister dying broke him. He's sick. And sick people heal, right?'

'No, don't do that Millie. Don't make excuses for him. He knows right from wrong and what he is doing is inexcusable.'

With a trembling hand, she dabs at her tears. Her head bobs in a half-hearted nod, a fragile gesture of agreement. Her eyes tell a different story. She doesn't believe me, and I grasp her hand tighter, willing my assurance to awaken her belief in what I'm saying.

Images of her blood-spattered bathroom refuse to leave me alone. I *have* to know what happened. I have to save her. 'Tell me, Millie. Has he hurt you lately? Physically?'

She shakes her head. Too quickly to be the truth.

'Millie, please. You can talk to me.'

'I can't do this. I need to go.'

Millie rises to leave and I stand with her. I reach out, my fingers encircling her wrist in a gentle but firm grasp. With a slight tug, I turn her around to face me, our eyes locking. To my horror, she winces and pulls back, leaving my hand hanging in the air.

'Millie, please. I will never hurt you. Can't you see what he's doing to you?' My voice is low, urgent, a fierce whisper that cuts through the silence. A whimper escapes her lips at the stark reality of her situation. 'Millie, you can trust me.'

To my surprise, she takes a step forward and presses her chest against my towering frame. I tremble at the intimacy.

'How did you become so kind?' she asks, tracing a finger along my cheek. I can feel her trembling, too. I close my eyes, savouring her touch. 'Zack, I have never met a man like you. I have never felt kindness like this before. It's so confusing.' She cups my cheeks. 'It's scary.' Her breath is warm against my neck. I can only respond by drawing a deep breath. 'The world needs more men like you. There's just so much ... *darkness* out there.'

I scoff gently. That's quite a bold statement. Her hand caressing my cheek slides to the back of my head, and she pulls me closer. Her lips graze mine, the feather-light touch sending a shiver down my spine.

She smiles against my mouth, and I feel her teeth graze my lower lip. 'I think I've discovered your weak spot, Dr Briens.' She giggles, but her laughter is hesitant.

I know I should pull away. I should put a stop to this. Millie is vulnerable and I'm in a position of power. Her emotions are all over the place and there's a high chance she'll regret this afterwards, putting her in danger of confessing to Dexter. But her warmth draws me in and despite my better judgement, I lose myself in that tinkling laughter and pull her towards me. To my delight, she hops up and wraps her legs around my waist.

'I know you were outside my house the other week,' she whispers into my ear. 'And I know what you did.'

My eyes widen in horror. I stare into her eyes, not knowing what to say.

She giggles again, more sure this time, and squeezes her legs tighter. She runs her hand through my hair. 'Don't worry, Dr Briens. It was quite the turn-on.' She bites my ear lobe, moaning gently. 'It's been a while since someone has wanted me for *me*, and not just because I'm part of their twisted game. I think you're ... sexy.'

I lose all sense of control. I push her onto my desk. Pens and papers scatter all over the floor. Her dress rides up, exposing goddess thighs. Pulling her closer to me, I push my crotch against hers as our mouths clash in a kissing frenzy.

I'm hungry for her. *Starving*. I focus every one of my senses on this perfect woman who clutches me like she needs me as much as I need her. There is no longer an outside. There's just me and Millie and our little bubble.

Her hands run over my shoulders and down my back. They scoop over my ass and land on my crotch, clutching at my erect penis like it's her lifeline. I groan into her mouth and push her skirt up to reveal a tiny red thong. Her feminine scent ignites my centre and I growl. I press my face between her breasts and moan into their glory.

The sudden click of my office door opening shatters the moment and a tiny voice gasps. 'Daddy?'

CHAPTER 15

Georgia is standing in the doorway and Chelsea is behind her, mouth agape. 'Come on, honey. Why don't we go and watch some videos on my phone?' Chelsea coaxes my daughter away and shoots me a scowl as the door closes behind her.

I smooth out my clothes, muttering curses under my breath. Millie sits perched on the edge of my desk, legs crossed, her skirt still bunched up around her waist. Her face is crimson but she doesn't make a move to arrange her clothes.

'Well, that was bad timing,' she says, like my relationship with Georgia hasn't just shattered into a million pieces. 'Your receptionist was fuming.' She's clearly in shock. I can still see a triangle of her underwear between her legs and I internally beg her to put it away before my erection returns.

'Millie, you need to leave.' It saddens me to say it after the ecstasy we have just experienced, but I need to sort things out with my daughter.

Millie gives me a gentle smile and hops off my desk, smoothing down her clothes. 'I know. Good luck with your daughter, Zack. I'm so sorry. I have a tendency to screw everything up.' She presses a hand against my chest. 'I think I just got swept away. This won't happen again.'

'You haven't screwed this up,' I whisper. And it's the truth. This may not have been the best way for Georgia to learn about us, but at least it kick-starts the inevitable end of my marriage and the move to greener pastures. 'But if you really don't want this to happen again, I fully support that.' We both know I feel differently. My breath is still laboured with desire.

Now, more than ever, I am motivated to find a solution to my custody dilemma. I've been sitting still for far too long. I can see what I want and now I just have to find a way to get it.

I watch the sway of Millie's hips as she leaves. There's no sign of Chelsea or Georgia in the reception area, but the hum of the microwave gives away their whereabouts. I wait until the lift carrying Millie disappears to the floors below before I turn to face the consequences of my actions. I take a deep breath.

Chelsea looks up at me when I enter the cramped kitchenette. She's stirring hot chocolate into warmed milk for my precious girl, who won't even look in my direction. Georgia's cheeks redden under my gaze, and I can practically feel the heat emanating off them.

'What are you doing here?' I ask Chelsea.

'I left my wedding planning notes on my desk. And I came back to fetch them. I never thought I'd be seeing that!' Her drawn-on eyebrows lift.

I look away shamefully. 'Can I have a moment with Georgia, please?'

She squints at me, not knowing whether to leave us alone. Anger swells inside me. No matter what I did in my office, no matter what Georgia saw, I am Georgia's father and Chelsea has no say over whether I can be alone with her or not.

She eventually nods, setting the drink on the counter. 'Careful honey, it's hot,' she warns Georgia, running a hand over her hair. It's a heartwarming gesture.

Chelsea shoulders me as she leaves the room. The look she throws me contains pure loathing.

It saddens me that this might mean I have to say goodbye to the best damn receptionist I've ever had. But it's nothing compared to the fear I feel of Chelsea reporting me for breaching the code of ethics. I curse my lack of control. I should have locked the damn door.

'Georgia?' I kneel down to face her, but she refuses to make eye contact and turns her head away. 'What you saw in there ...'

'It's okay, Daddy. I know about sex.'

I choke back my shock. What disgusting sex ed lessons has Sarah been giving our innocent little girl? I make a mental note to have words with my wife.

'Okaaay,' I draw out the word as I try to make sense of what she's just said.

I brush past it for now. I need to focus on what matters right this minute. 'But that wasn't sex, darling. That was ...' I struggle to find the words to explain my loss of control to my six-year-old girl.

'Kissing?' she asks, finally meeting my gaze. Her eyes are brimming with tears.

'Yes. And I know that's naughty. I shouldn't be kissing anyone but your mummy. I know that. I was being silly.'

'But you and Mummy don't love each other anymore.' She speaks with such conviction it makes me flinch.

What kind of damage are we doing to this poor girl? I want to wrap her in my arms and tell her everything will be all right, but I can't bring myself to lie to her. Her face is the epitome of innocence. She deserves the truth.

'You're right, darling.' I squeeze her shoulder. 'I've been trying to make it work with Mummy, I really have, but sometimes things can be too broken to fix.'

'So, you kiss other ladies?'

I sigh. 'No. Just that one lady, that one time.' I don't want to tell Georgia it was a mistake. Not only would it be a lie, it would also tarnish Millie's perfection.

'Will you kiss her again, Daddy?'

I shrug. I honestly don't know. Do I want to kiss Millie again? Without a doubt. But I have no clue how Millie feels about it all. She must be so confused right now.

'All I know right now, Georgie, is that we can't tell Mummy about this. I need to figure things out.' I need to not fuel the fire of my wife's vindictiveness. Who knows what she's truly capable of?

'Because it'll make her sad?'

I nod. 'Exactly. And we don't want to make her sad, do we? I'll sort things out with Mummy, I promise. In a way that won't make her sad. I just need to have a long think about it first.'

She chews her lip as she ponders the dilemma. We've spent years teaching her that lying is bad. Now that seems like a ridiculous notion. Georgia is a good girl; can she break the rules for me?

'I don't want to make her sad, no.' She shakes her head resolutely. 'But Daddy, you should tell her the truth. It's important to be honest.'

Everything is so black and white to Georgia. Tell the truth and all will be okay. Maybe she's on to something. If I tell Sarah, I can finally release the chain she has around my neck. I just need to put some things in place first.

'I will. I promise,' I say, brushing a strand of hair away from her sweet face. 'I will make this right. But I need some time to figure out the best way. Do you think you can do that for me? Can you give me a bit of time?'

She draws in a deep breath and her eyes dart to the cooling hot chocolate. I pick it up and offer it to her. 'Can you do that for me?' I repeat.

She nods, accepting the drink. 'Yes, Daddy.'

'That's my girl. I love you.' I press a kiss to the top of her head.

CHAPTER 16

We head home without talking. I play that dreadful Taylor Swift song that Georgia loves so much, to try and put the events of the afternoon out of her mind. It seems to work – she's mouthing along to the lyrics, pretending she's in a music video without a care in the world. As soon as we enter the house, she goes straight to her bedroom whilst I work through my guilt for what I have just asked Georgia to do by avoiding Sarah.

I wait with bated breath as I hear Sarah go upstairs to greet Georgia. I can hear them chatting, the tone light and easy, but it isn't until Sarah comes downstairs and continues to ignore me that I relax my shoulders. Georgia kept her promise. If she had spilled the beans, Sarah would be gunning for blood.

I celebrate by imagining Millie's kiss pressing on me and I run my fingers across my tender bottom lip where she nibbled at me. Despite the stress of Georgia catching us, the memory may be one of the best of my life. And one I intend to experience again and again.

Desperation to see Millie again takes over any feelings of shame, and I text her.

The next day, she approaches me at a gentle pace. The evening sun is searingly bright and I cup my hand over my eyes to provide shade from the glare. 'Zack?' Millie is now standing outside my car, leaning on the driver's-side door, peering through the open window.

Horrified by what I see, I reach out to touch her. There's a dark, mottled bruise surrounding her left eye and extending to her hairline. Fury surges through my veins. I long to absorb her pain and it takes every ounce of my self-restraint not to drive to her house right now and end Dexter's sad, pathetic life.

'He did this yesterday? After you came to see me?' The words tumble from my lips as guilt pours through me. This is my fault. If I hadn't taken her out of her routine yesterday, Dexter wouldn't have gotten mad at her.

Millie nods at me and a sad smile flitters across her face. 'Don't blame yourself,' she reads my mind. 'Only I know what he's truly capable of. I chose to come to you yesterday; it was *my* fault.'

I slam my hands on the steering wheel. All composure has slipped away. 'Fuck Dexter! He can't do this to you.'

To Millie's credit, she doesn't recoil at my anger and I am pleased to realise she doesn't fear me. She nods along. 'I know that, Zack. But it isn't that easy.'

I yearn to draw her closer to me. And never let her go. Instead, I say, 'Where does he think you are now? Do you have time for a coffee?'

She catches me off guard with a grin, a wicked glint in her eye. 'He's away with work.' Her lips press together. 'Fancy a cocktail instead?'

One cocktail turns into two, and by eleven o'clock it's closer to ten. I feel giddy and elated to spend time in Millie's company. She's a breath of fresh air, laughing with glee, pulling me up to dance, buying shots of tequila. I feel young again. Free.

We kiss in hidden corners of the bar, our hands exploring each other. I'm in heaven. And undoubtedly in love with this woman.

Overwhelmed by emotion and dizzy from a few drinks too many, I need fresh air. I pull her to a free table by the open door. Her cheeks are flushed and in the dim light, the bruising is no longer visible. She looks so youthful and jubilant and it makes my heart sing.

'We need to talk,' I blurt out, my words laced with urgency. I consciously mould my expression into one of genuine concern, desperate for her to grasp the gravity of what I'm about to say, but I fail miserably, and she laughs at my twisted features.

'What's going on, Zack?' Her words aren't slurring quite as badly as mine.

I swallow the burp that's threatening to ruin the moment. I take her hand between both of mine. 'You can't carry on like this.'

She presses her lips together as she looks into my eyes. 'Zack, we're friends right now. Can't we save the therapy for the office?'

I search for the words to speak the truth without frightening her away. 'Millie, you're not a usual client to me. I'm ...' The truth of telling her I love her flirts with my tongue, but I push it away. I'm far too drunk for that. She'll never believe me whilst I'm in this state and I curse my inability to handle alcohol. 'I'm concerned about you.'

She pulls her hand away from mine and gently rests it on her lap. 'Surely you're concerned about all of your clients? It's part of your job. So why are you here, with me? What's going on here, Zack?'

She knows exactly why I'm here. No, her situation isn't unusual or shocking; it's sadly very normal to me. What's special in this case is so obviously *her*.

I sigh and turn to stare out the huge windows spanning the front of the bar. Outside, a woman is crying as she searches for something inside her handbag. She's alone, most probably abandoned by her partner. Women deserve so much better.

I can feel myself swaying so I straighten myself out, only to lean too far the other way and almost fall from my chair.

Millie giggles. 'Come on. Why so serious all of a sudden? I thought we were having fun?'

'Oh, we are. There's just something you need to know.' I pause.

She waits for the big revelation, her eyebrows raised.

'You've got to end it with Dexter.'

She sighs with exasperation and rolls her eyes.

'No, Millie, you have to listen to me. Look, last year I had a client – Katie. I so desperately tried to get her to leave her marriage, but she point-blank refused. She stayed with him. And you know what happened to her?'

She shakes her head slowly, tears pooling in the corners of her eyes. 'No.' It's barely a whisper.

'She died, Millie. Her husband stabbed her nine times in the stomach. She didn't even put up a fight.'

Millie presses her hands to her face and shakes her head as my story hits close to home. A sob escapes her perfect lips.

I gently pull her hands away so I can look her in the eyes. 'I'm sorry, Millie. But I cannot let that happen again. I cannot let that happen to *you*. This world needs you in it. *I* need you.'

We stare into each other's eyes, imploring each other to try and understand what we're both going through. I know she wants to pretend everything is okay. But I know how he treats her. I know how much he hurts her. There's no way out of this and I know if I don't put an end to it, she will keep going back to him. Until she's dead.

I will not let that happen. If it means Millie dying, then I know what I need to do to prevent that from happening.

'What would you do in my situation?' she asks me. Her hands are trembling as she pushes her hair out of her eyes. She looks at me all doe-eyed, her full lips puckered. 'What do I do, Zack?'

'That's what I am trying to tell you. You don't need to do anything.'

'What do you mean?'

'Just say the word and I will do it all for you. I will remove the problem.'

She laughs, manically slamming her palms on the table. 'Oh, come on, Zack! You're being dramatic. You're acting like you're going to kill him.'

I stare at her, my eyes imploring.

She stutters, 'You were being dramatic …'

'Just say the word, Millie. And Dexter will never hurt you again.'

Her eyes widen and she takes a deep breath. She's left him before and got dragged straight back in. She knows there's only one way out for good. And I know I have the means to do it.

We sit staring at each other. She's panting, and I'm holding my breath.

'Okay,' she nods. 'It's time to end this.'

Chapter 17

The pounding in my head is merciless, a relentless throb that grows more intense by the second. I attempt to open my eyes, but the searing sunlight seeping through the cracks of my eyelids pierces my skull. I squeeze my eyes shut again, but the pain in my head remains.

As a stupid teenager I had my fair share of hangovers, but this is on a whole other level. A groan escapes my lips as I try to shift my weight, my ass muscles screaming in protest. Why did I have to fall asleep sitting up?

As I sit here, desperately trying to gather my bearings, a wave of nausea crashes over me, threatening to spew the copious amounts of alcohol sloshing around in my stomach. The taste in my mouth is vile, a revolting mixture of stale booze and kebab. My parched throat is too dry to swallow it down and my stomach tenses in a dry retch.

I reach out in front of me, seeking something to steady myself against the spinning sensation, and my hand collides with a cold, hard surface. Instinctively, I grip onto it, the sudden jolt forcing my eyes open. Confusion floods my mind as I find myself sitting in the driver's seat of my own car.

Blinking rapidly, I try to make sense of where I am. I'm surrounded by grey concrete and a few cars, and a slope to my right reaches down to the level below. I'm in a multi-storey car park. The sun is high over the horizon, its rays casting an eerie glow on the concrete space.

How did I get here? I wasn't parked here before I met Millie last night. A flashback flitters across the forefront of my mind. Fumbling for my keys, dropping them multiple times before finally pushing the button with furious frustration to unlock the doors.

Did I seriously drive that drunk? It's a miracle I'm still alive. Dread slams down into the bottom of my stomach. Did I do anything stupid last night?

'Millie?' I mumble as my memories of last night start to appear. I close my eyes and concentrate on the gaps in my memory, desperately trying to piece together the fragments of images that come to me from the night before.

Millie's face materialises in my mind's eye. She's cheekily smiling over a shot of tequila, her eyes twinkling with the glow of nightclub lights. 'To the future!' she toasted, before we swiftly tipped back the toxic liquid, letting it burn a path down our throats. But even through her cheerful façade, I remember the glimmer of fear in her eyes, her apprehension about the decision we had made.

In that moment, we sought solace in the numbing effects of alcohol, desperately trying to make sense of the seriousness of the decision we had made.

'Urrgghh,' I groan now. The only time I ever drink now is a sherry with Dad at Christmas, so it's no wonder that the amount of alcohol I consumed last night has left me feeling like death warmed up. My body hates me right now. I hate me, too.

I have a vague memory of dancing, the alcohol having washed away the guilt of what I'd agreed to do for Millie. She turned off her phone, no longer caring about Dexter's wrath. A commitment to the plan.

Did I really tell her I was going to kill Dexter? She must have known I was lying. I would never hurt a soul. It was the alcohol talking. She must have known that. It was all just a silly game. A fantasy. A representation of what Millie's life *could* be like if Dexter was no longer in it. I feel embarrassed by my words. By my drunken intentions.

Through my haze, I can still feel Millie's body pressed against mine as we danced and I can't suppress the smile that tugs at the corners of my mouth. With Millie last night, I experienced a sense of euphoria that I haven't felt in a long time. Her presence has a way of drawing out a side of me that I thought had been lost. With her, laughter comes effortlessly – that deep, belly-aching laughter that hurts. It's ecstasy and I'm addicted.

That's what I want for the next *forever*. Maybe Dexter's death is the best option. Just not by my hand. I shudder at the thought of taking a man's life.

Where is Millie now?

Motivated into action, I frantically search around the car for my phone. After a few moments of scrabbling around, I find it lying screen-down on the rear seat footwell.

As I pick up the phone and tap the screen to life, I'm greeted by a slew of notifications – nine missed calls and a single text message. With a mix of curiosity and apprehension, I open the text first, only to find it's from Sarah. Attached is a selfie of Georgia, my little girl, with a beaming smile that shows a newly missing tooth. The pure joy and pride radiating from her face is infectious, and despite my current sorry state, I can't help but grin along with her.

I notice that among the missed calls, there's one from Mum. She's left a message: 'Hi, darling. Just checking in with you. Just so you know, I didn't make it 'round to yours last night. Your Dad was poorly. Anyway, I called Sarah and she said all was fine.'

Annoyed at Mum for not doing as I wished, worried for my dad and his deteriorating health, and angry at Sarah for being ... well, Sarah ... I turn back to my phone to push away the negative thoughts I'm too hungover to deal with right now.

I have three messages from Chelsea: the first asking if I am okay and wondering when I will be in the office, the second obviously getting annoyed, and the third telling me she's rescheduled all of today's appointments and desperately asking me to call her back so she knows I'm okay. I send her a quick message to let her know I'm ill and to thank her for rescheduling.

Then I turn my attention to the remaining missed calls, all of which are from Millie. My heart skips a beat as I realise that all missed calls were in the past hour. Did Dexter find out about last night? Is Millie okay?

I feel sick with worry as I tap on my phone to listen to the voicemail messages she has left me. A sense of unease creeps over me. Each message follows a similar pattern, her voice growing more and more frantic with every call.

'Zack. It's me. Where the hell did you go last night?? We need to talk.'

In her final message, she informs me that she's heading to my office to look for me, her voice wracked with desperation.

I jam my key into the ignition and throw my car into reverse. The tires screech as I manoeuvre out of the car park.

***

As I burst into the reception area, still donning yesterday's clothes and reeking of stale alcohol, Chelsea's eyebrow shoots up in surprise. 'There you are! Everything okay, Dr Briens?'

'I'm fine. Sorry I'm late,' I say, my tone harsher than intended as I stride purposefully towards my office, eager to avoid any further questioning.

Chelsea leans forward in her seat, her gaze fixed on me as she continues. 'It's just that before I rescheduled your other clients, I had to send Hazel Dyer home. You were forty minutes late for her appointment.' She looks furious with me.

Her words hit me like a punch to the gut. I'm never late for appointments, and the fact I've let down a patient due to my own personal issues fills me with a sense of shame and self-reproach. Not to mention the difficult position I put Chelsea in. I silently vow to assess her salary once I've found out what's wrong with Millie. Maybe it's time Chelsea got a raise.

As I turn to fully face Chelsea, my dishevelled appearance seems to catch her off guard. 'Are you really sick?' she asks with raised eyebrows. She presses her tongue to the inside of her cheek and there's a questioning glint in her eye. 'I find pizza helps when I'm *hungover*,' she continues. 'I could order you a delivery?'

Her offer, though well-intentioned, only serves to make my stomach roll. The idea of greasy pizza is far from appealing, and I can't help but grimace. 'No, thanks, I'll be fine. Have you seen ...'

'Emily O'Neale? Yes, she's been in your office for the last five minutes. I tried to make her wait out here, but she was very insistent. Maybe she's waiting for round two ...' She returns to her computer screen, leaving the accusation hanging in the air.

Chelsea's cheek irks me. I understand I have put her in a difficult position this morning, but her lack of tact is massively disappointing. I expected better from her. I contemplate pleading innocence, but truth be told, my extramarital activities have nothing to do with Chelsea.

When I enter my office, Millie immediately spins to face me with a scowl on her face. 'Where did you go last night?' Her tone catches me off guard. She's furious and I don't know why. What have I done wrong?

'I was with you last night. What's wrong?' I don't tell her I have no idea what happened after we left the club, or how I ended up in my car at the complete opposite end of town.

'No, Zack. I went to the toilet and when I came back, you were gone. Tell me where you went.'

I stutter before throwing my hands in the air. 'I have no idea,' I admit. 'I can't remember.'

Millie takes a step closer to me, ferocity radiating from her. Her eyes bore into mine as she accuses, 'You went to my house, didn't you?'

The question hangs in the air, heavy with implications. The sudden shift in her demeanour and the intensity of her gaze leaves me stunned, my mind scrambling to make sense of everything. I try to search my hazy memory for any recollection of going to Millie's house. But the truth is, I have no idea where I went last night. I can't recall any details of what I did. It's just grisly black.

Surely I'd remember going to Millie's house. And why would I just leave her alone in the club? Nothing is making sense and it's making my head spin. 'No, I didn't go to yours,' I say, but my voice wobbles with doubt. 'Millie, what's going on?'

She sighs and turns her back to me. I realise she's wearing the same clothes as last night too, only she's thrown a thick, black jumper on top. 'Look, I know what we agreed last night, but you didn't think I actually meant it, did you?' She spins back around and jabs me in the chest. 'You didn't honestly think I wanted Dexter *dead*?'

The room is spinning fast now. I want to run away from this horror show, but at the same time I desperately need to pull Millie close to reassure her that everything is going to be okay.

Of course I didn't mean it. Millie must know that. We were just having fun with the idea. A bit of dark humour.

'Millie, I have no intention of hurting Dexter. You must know that.'

My panic heightens as she stays silent and tears start to roll down her cheeks. She shakes her head at me. 'You did it, didn't you? Zack, you weren't supposed to actually do it!'

I step back from her flailing arms. 'I didn't do anything!' I protest. She comes at me, and I grab her shoulders in an attempt to calm her down, but she pummels at my chest, forcing my hands away.

'Bullshit!' she screams, the volume making me wince. 'There's blood everywhere, Zack. Everywhere!'

I pull away with shock. 'Millie, I honestly don't know what you're talking about ... I thought Dexter was away? What blood?'

Millie just backs away towards the door, a keening sound escaping her throat. 'I love him, Zack. He might not be perfect, but I love him.' She opens the door to find Chelsea standing behind it, her hand raised like she's about to knock. 'And you've taken all of that away from me.'

Millie flees my office, taking the stairs instead of waiting for the lift.

I blink away the horror of what's just happened, trying to force a sense of clarity to the situation. I may have planned to kill Dexter, but I didn't do it. *Did I?* Shit. I wish I could remember what happened last night.

'Everything okay, Dr Briens?' Chelsea asks. She looks pale. I wonder how much she heard through the thick wooden door.

'Everything is just fine,' I lie, glancing down to avoid her probing gaze.

But everything is not fine. My heart is beating so hard it feels like it's pushing its way out of my chest.

CHAPTER 18

My car flies down the road, chasing Millie's. We hurtle past a
school and the children on the playground point at the two
idiots driving way too fast. The sharp turns take my breath away as I
refuse to hit the brakes. I need answers. Now.

We pull up outside her house, my car behind hers in the driveway.
As she approaches her front door, she throws me a glare over her
shoulder. Coming here was a silly idea. I blame morbid curiosity – I
need to see what Millie was talking about.

What has happened to make her so shaken up?

Millie reaches the house first and lets the door swing shut in my
face. I clutch the door handle and take a deep breath before pushing
open the door. Being here legitimately ignites my guilt at breaking in
all those weeks ago.

I freeze. I can't do this. It's my job to embolden those who have
lost all sense of self-identity, but I have never felt so lost. I don't know
what is happening and I don't know my role in all this. Whatever is
on the other side of this door feels too big. I've become too involved.

My relationship with Millie has crossed boundaries that I should never have even stepped towards, and this is my punishment.

But, Millie ... I need to be there for her. I owe her that.

I step inside to find Millie standing in the hallway, facing me with her arms crossed. The look on her face is thunderous. We lock gazes for a few moments before she whirls around and walks further into the house. The pristine hallway shows no sign of any struggle and there's no blood. I doubt the severity of the situation as Millie presented it in my office. Maybe this isn't as bad as she first thought. Maybe she exaggerated? I pray internally I'm right, but I know delusion when I see it.

I throw all those thoughts aside when I enter the living room. Her once immaculate cream carpets are defiled with murky, rust-coloured stains. A bucket of pink-tinged water and tattered rags lay nearby, evidence of Millie's futile attempts to scrub the nightmare away.

'Millie,' I begin carefully, 'you tried cleaning it?'

'I panicked! I didn't know what to do and cleaning the mess felt like the only sensible option. But the more I cleaned, the angrier I got,' she spits, transfixed by the stains. 'Did you kill him, Zack? Did you kill Dexter?'

I can feel my frustration mounting and I scowl at her. Why won't she believe me? 'I told you, I didn't lay a finger on him!'

'Don't you dare get pissed at me! Is that the same temper that made you attack him?'

I roll my eyes back and sigh. 'I never touched him. After our conversation last night, this looks suspicious, I get that, but you've got to believe me. I was with you last night.'

'Until you weren't!' she hisses venomously. 'Where did you go after the bar?'

I shrug helplessly. 'I just know that I didn't come here. I'm sure of it.'

Millie crumples, her anguished sobs making her tiny frame jolt. 'I didn't want this. Yes, we had our problems, but I never actually wanted *this*.' She kneels into the soggy carpet, staining her knees, and motions at the red mess in front of us. 'What we discussed was just a silly fantasy. I was being silly. I love him, Zack! You weren't supposed to go ahead with it!'

Disgust twists in my stomach. How do these sick men wield so much control over their victims? How much more does she have to endure before seeing sense? I don't know what happened here, or even if Dexter was involved. But if he was, I can categorically say he deserved it. Bad things should happen to bad people. And I'm not a bad person.

I reach out to comfort her, but she recoils violently. 'Don't! Don't you dare touch me,' she warns, her voice quaking.

'Please, Millie. You have to trust me.'

'Trust you?' she barks. 'How? How can I possibly trust you?'

She moves to pick up the blood-soaked cloth, but I intercept her. 'Wait. Don't touch anything else. We need to call the police.'

Her face blanches. 'What? No.'

I squat down to face her and grip her arms, pulling her upright. I need to make her see sense. In the midst of her panic, she's not thinking straight.

'Millie, if you don't believe me, then the police will have to prove my innocence,' I say, though doubt niggles at my core. Although I am mostly sure I didn't do this, I cannot categorically say I didn't come here last night. I follow my instincts on this and pray I'm right. We need to get the police involved.

She nods enthusiastically, her eyes darting back to the stain. I pull my phone out of my pocket. As I type the second nine, she stops me in my tracks. 'You know you're going to prison for this, don't you?'

Heat drains from my body. 'No, I won't. I can't. I didn't do anything wrong.'

'Really? Well, I hope you've got a bloody good alibi.' Her lips curl in disgust.

I tap the button to cancel my call. 'Millie, you've got to believe me. I didn't do anything. I help people, not hurt them.' I look around the room in a pathetic attempt to find something to prove my innocence. 'That's a lot of blood, right?' I step towards her but she darts backwards. 'You'd think if I was involved in this, I would have blood on me, too.'

She scans me up and down, from my white shirt to camel-coloured chinos and lastly my loafers. Finally, she makes eye contact. I see a glimmer of doubt cross her face and relief washes over me.

'What the fuck is going on?' she whispers.

I want to reach out to her but I refrain, not wanting to make things worse. 'And Millie, if I did do this, do you really believe I'd be suggesting you tell the police?'

She crumbles, a tear rolling down her cheek. 'I'm so confused,' she whispers, a broken woman. She sways on her feet. I catch her before she falls and her body sags against my chest.

In that moment, it's like I can finally breathe. Everything feels unequivocally right, as if I was destined to do this. To have this incredible woman in my arms. Cherish her. Worship her. As she weeps, I tentatively stroke her wild hair, matted from her frenzied clean of the carpets.

'Millie. I know this is hard, but, assuming this was Dexter, maybe this is your chance to break free of him. Maybe you can now build the life you deserve.' *With me.*

'It must have been him. Who else would be in the house? But, you don't understand,' she whimpers, her face buried into my chest. 'He was mine. He wasn't supposed to leave me.'

Inhaling her intoxicating scent, I murmur into her hair. 'Maybe it's time to demand better.' She nods against my thundering heart. She needs to see the truth.

'I told you about Katie, didn't I?'

She peers up with glistening, wide eyes. 'The woman who was killed?' There's a glint in her eye. My story is too stark against the backdrop of whatever massacre has occurred here. The poor girl looks terrified.

'Yes. She was special, like you. And Katie's death nearly destroyed me.' A sob works its way up my throat. 'I'm so relieved Dexter might be gone. He can't hurt you anymore.'

Her lips flatten into a grim line. 'You're a good man, aren't you, Zack?'

I press her to me once more. We can only hope Dexter is gone for good. I pray he really is dead.

And that I didn't kill him.

CHAPTER 19

'How's it going?' Dad's question makes me cringe. My marriage is on the brink of collapse, Georgia is withdrawing more and more every day, and work is terrible. Since the incident with Millie, I haven't been able to focus on my patients and I felt it only fair that I delayed all appointments until my head was in a better state. It also felt prudent to give Chelsea a few days off. I need to keep her sweet now that I've tarnished her opinion of me. I need someone on my side.

Leaving Millie in that blood-stained house killed me. She looked so lost, so alone; but she was adamant I leave, and obviously unsure about how to feel around me. I don't blame her. I don't know how to feel about myself either.

I force myself back to the present and look at Dad. He looks terrible. It's like he's deteriorating in front of our eyes. His dominant presence is wearing away.

'Have you been to see a doctor yet?' I ask him.

'Don't try to change the subject,' he snaps, trying to divert the attention off him.

'No, he hasn't,' cuts in Mum, placing a tray in front of us containing a pot of tea and a packet of Jaffa Cakes. 'I keep telling him. But he doesn't listen.'

'Theresa, don't talk about me as if I'm not here, please.'

Mum tuts and leaves the room. She looks tired, too. I can see the concern written in the wrinkles on her forehead.

'Now, tell me about work.' Dad heaves his body forward to make himself a cup of tea, but he immediately starts panting and I take over. He settles back into his chair.

'There's not much to say,' I lie. The truth is, I feel like everything I have worked so hard for is disintegrating. I'm ignoring my other patients as I am one hundred percent focused on Millie and the worry I feel about never clawing back our relationship.

I need a plan to get it together before my clients seek help elsewhere. Or worse, give up on their treatment. I bristle with disappointment, desperately trying to force away the feeling of shame.

Dad looks at me with his all-knowing eye. 'You've always been a shit liar, Zack,' he says. 'What's her name this time?'

I squeeze my eyes shut so I can't see his accusatory stare. 'There's nothing to worry about, Dad.'

'Bullshit!' he shouts, finally losing patience with me. 'Tell me the fucking truth, Zack! I ain't got time for this shit.' His brash tone takes me aback. Dad is usually so gentle and this version is downright terrifying. He only ever gets this mad when we've really messed up.

I want to bury myself in the sofa cushions and never come out. I hate it when Dad makes me feel like I never passed puberty. I feel like a naughty schoolboy who's been caught glancing up girls' skirts in the science lab. 'Her name's Millie,' I mumble. I open my eyes to face Dad's look of disgust. 'But there's nothing going on. I swear.'

And that's the truth. I haven't seen or heard from Millie since she found the splatters of blood on the floor. I have spent each evening sitting outside her house in case Dexter shows up and Millie needs my help. But the longer I wait, the more convinced I am that Dexter is dead.

Dad sighs at me and I'm stunned. I fully expected him to blow up at my confession, but it's like he's just too tired. Or he's given up on me. 'Oh, Zack,' he mutters, turning away from me. 'How many more times are you going to do this?'

'None,' I admit. Millie is the only one for me. If I can't have her, I'm not interested in anyone. I'm stuck in my miserable life forever.

'You've said that before. Why should I believe you this time?'

'It's the truth, Dad,' I implore. 'There's nothing to worry about.'

He takes a sip of his tea, glaring at me over the cup. 'I'm not going to be around forever, Zack. I can't keep seeing you make the same mistakes over and over.'

His defeated tone raises my eyebrows. He's weak, all energy drained out of him, and I can only blame my indiscretions. Dad is morphing into a stranger and it's terrifying.

My mind shifts to alarming extremes. I think of Mum and what would happen if Dad were to die. It would destroy her. Dad is all she knows and if he really is sick, she must be petrified.

I shake the thought away. No, Dad isn't dying. He's far too young. The stress I'm under is making me paranoid and emotional and I need to be careful I don't feed him the same.

'I've just got one thing to say to you, boy.' He pauses. 'Don't forget what happened to Katie. What you did to that poor woman. And don't forget what it did to you.'

Tears spring to my eyes. Katie was so sweet and kind. She married a man who played with her innocence and the day after Katie and I slept together for the first time, she was found lying on her bed, dead.

When the police came to enquire about my and Katie's relationship, I barely held it together. My grief was too huge. Whilst I recovered I had to shut the practice for three weeks and I lost my previous receptionist because I couldn't afford to pay her. The stress was almost too much to bear, so I can appreciate Dad's reservations. But it's different this time. Millie is worth all that.

Poor Katie. She deserved so much better. She was beautifully innocent and gorgeously honest. I can only assume her honesty forced her to confess her infidelity, and her bastard husband punished her by stabbing her nine times in the abdomen.

Her death is on my hands, and that kills me to this day.

CHAPTER 20

Since Dexter disappeared, I've been living on tenterhooks.

I pull up into my driveway, bracing myself for the sight of police pounding on my front door. If Millie truly believes I laid a finger on Dexter, there's no doubt in my mind she'll report me to the police.

When I left Millie that day, I was so sure she believed that I didn't do it, but as time slips by and my messages to Millie continue to go ignored, doubt is creeping in. Either she knows deep down I didn't touch the guy and she just needs some space, or she thinks I seriously hurt Dexter. My hopeful side is praying Millie just needs some space to think things through and with space will come clarity. She'll realise she's better off without Dexter. She'll know for sure that I'm the man for her.

As I step inside my home, an eerie stillness greets me, the only sound being the low, steady hum of the fridge. Making my way to the kitchen, I grab a glass and fill it to the brim with water. Dad's words play on my mind, giving me a headache that feels like it's trying to push my eardrums out of my skull.

After months of self-reflection I came to realise that Katie's death, despite breaking my heart, was not my fault. I tried to help her; I wanted to tear her away from her husband. How was I to know he'd flip out and kill her?

A sob bursts out of me and with trembling hands I drink the glass of water in an attempt to wash away the immense guilt that will plague me forever.

The guilt I feel for Katie has never left me and I'm scared that guilt made my drunk self act out. I wrack my brain, trying to piece together the fragments of the night I went out drinking with Millie. I was flying high that night, that much I can be certain about. Millie and I were having a blast. Was I so caught up in a state of bliss that I decided to act on our oath to end Dexter's life? It was just a twisted game, not something I actually went through with. Right?

'Fuck!' I yell, slamming my glass down.

The shrill ring of the doorbell shatters my train of thought. I grumble further curse words as I make my way to the front door. I yank the door open, ready to give my visitor a piece of my mind.

'Aaron?' His name leaves my lips, dripping with the contempt he deserves. I'm in no fit state to deal with his shit right now. 'What do you want?'

'Zack, a pleasure as always,' he quips, brushing past me without invitation and striding into the living room like he owns the place.

'Look, Aaron, I'm really not in the mood for your crap today,' I announce as I trail after him, ready to give him an earful. But the words die on my tongue when I see him slumped on my couch, hunched over with his head cradled in his hands. The sight stops me in my tracks. 'What's going on with you now?'

'All right, Zack. You don't need to sound so fucking judgemental.'

'Judgemental? I only asked how you are.'

He brings his hands up to rest on the top of his head. 'Didn't sound like it. You're always fucking judging me.'

'Seriously, did you come all the way here just to pick a fight? I've got enough on my goddamn plate as it is, Aaron.' I cross my arms, my jaw clenched tight as I stare him down, waiting for an explanation. The tension in the room is like a lead weight hanging over us, and I can feel my patience wearing thinner by the second.

'Ever stop to consider that maybe, just maybe, I need my big brother right now?' He lifts his head, his eyes boring into mine with an intensity that catches me off guard. 'For a guy with so many fancy letters after your name, you're pretty damn clueless when it comes to reading people.'

I stand there, my jaw hanging open at my brother's insult. This is too much. I can't cope with this, not now. It doesn't take a genius to see that Aaron needs help, but the truth is, I'm in way over my head. His demons run too deep, and the thought of prying open that Pandora's box terrifies me. Right now, I'm not in a fit state to face whatever darkness he's grappling with.

I know I've been a piss-poor excuse for a brother. But, then again, so has he. I've always felt that being a shit brother was justified when the other party vehemently refuses help. And now, as he sits there practically begging for my help, I can't bring myself to give a damn. There's just too much bad blood between us, too many years of resentment. He'll have to find someone else to help him.

He shakes his head, frustrated by my silence, and stands up, looming over me. 'Things have just been spiralling out of control. Trust me, if I had anywhere else to go, I wouldn't be here. It's not like I can go to Dad.'

'I can smell the booze on you,' I say, turning my head away from the overpowering stench of whiskey on his breath.

He lets out a harsh laugh. 'There's that judgemental prick again.'

We stand there, locked in a silent stare-down, both of us trying to figure out our next move. Deep down I know, in his own messed up way, Aaron's here to extend an olive branch. And for a fleeting moment, I consider reaching out, cautiously accepting his peace offering, but I can't. Not now, not with everything blowing up on me.

'Look, I don't know what you're going through, but I can't do this. Not now.' I shake my head at him. 'I'm sorry.'

My apology makes his eyes grow wide. The whites of his eyes are stained red. He exhales heavily, his shoulders sagging as if they're carrying the weight of the world. 'It's fine,' he mumbles.

He turns to leave but freezes when the doorbell chimes once more. A chill runs down my spine. This is it – Millie has called the police. They're here to fill in the blanks of my drunken escapades, slap cuffs on my wrists, and haul me away.

'Aren't you going to get that?' Aaron asks, but I'm rooted to the spot.

With a tut of annoyance, he strides to the door. I turn my back, bracing myself for the inevitable as he swings it open. 'Yes?' he barks at the visitors, his tone harsh and confrontational. I cringe, wishing he wouldn't antagonise the police when they're about to arrest me.

To my surprise, a timid voice responds. 'Hello, sir. How are you today?'

I spin around to see a small woman standing on my doorstep, clutching a stack of leaflets. To her credit, despite being dwarfed by my brother's intimidating demeanour, she seems unfazed by his gruff tone. 'Have you ever considered the afterlife?' she begins, but before she can continue, Aaron slams the door in her face. Through the frosted glass, we watch her retreating figure fade into the distance.

'Afterlife my arse. Apparently I'm destined for hell.' Aaron laughs, a bitter edge to his voice. 'The devil won't know what hit him.'

I feel awful. How dare Aaron treat an innocent woman like that? How did he become so rude?

More importantly, though, Millie hasn't gone to the police. Maybe she did believe me? Relief floods through me, my heart pounding in my chest. My flip-flop of worry and determination that I'm innocent is absolutely shattering and I don't think I can do this anymore.

Screw her silence. I need to talk to Millie. I need to get to her now. My sudden urge to see her intensifies at a roaring speed.

I turn to my brother. 'Now you can get out,' I growl at Aaron, my patience gone. Why is he still here, lingering awkwardly, wringing his hands? Does he not know I have better things to do?

'What?' He looks at me, confused at my sudden change in tone.

His moronic look makes something inside of me snap. 'Get out!' I roar, hurling myself at him with a sudden, explosive force. The impact catches him off guard, and we both crash to the floor at the bottom of the stairs, a tangle of limbs.

My recent anguish pours out of me and the violence releases every negative feeling I have. I ram into Aaron again. He's become Dexter; he's every drop of fear I have felt for every client I've seen since opening my practice. He's my scapegoat for every nasty feeling I have absorbed from each of my clients.

Aaron tries to push me away but I slam my shoulder into him again. He lets out a cry of pain as his side slams against the bottom step, the sound echoing through the house. For a moment, I'm stunned by my own actions and the violence that seems to have come out of nowhere.

'Fucking hell, Zack. What's got into you?'

Without bothering to respond, I rear back and drive my fist into his face with all the force I can muster. To my surprise, he barely flinches, absorbing the blow like it's nothing. He grabs my head in retaliation, and slams it against the wall with a sickening thud.

The world turns momentarily black.

In an instant, we're grappling on the floor, trading blows like we're kids again, pummelling each other with a fury borne by years of pent-up resentment and anger.

We're so caught up in our brawl that we don't hear the front door open.

'Zack!' Sarah screams out. I look up but I only see Georgia peeking at me from behind Sarah's thick thighs. She's clutching her beloved bear, Hugsy.

'What on Earth is happening here?' Sarah screeches, her voice shrill with disbelief and anger. She quickly pulls Georgia away, shielding my little girl with her body.

I pull away from Aaron, and we both slump against the wall, sitting on the floor like a pair of misbehaving schoolboys caught red-handed by the headmaster.

'I'm so sorry, honey,' I say, my voice soft and filled with guilt. I try to reach out to Georgia, desperate to reassure her, but Sarah swats my hand away, her eyes ablaze.

'Georgia, why don't you go upstairs and get changed out of your school uniform?' Sarah suggests. Georgia hesitates, glancing at me uncertainly before heading upstairs, carefully stepping over the splatter of blood on the carpet.

As soon as we hear her bedroom door shut, Sarah rounds on me. 'What the hell do you think you're doing?!'

Aaron hangs his head in shame, but I couldn't care less about Sarah's opinion of me right now. 'Why is Georgia home from school early?' I ask her.

She scoffs. 'That is not what we're talking about right now.'

'You don't get to dictate what I can and can't talk about. What's wrong with my daughter?' I demand, my voice firm.

Sarah glares at me, her fury turning her cheeks red.

'I'd better go,' Aaron mumbles, clambering to his feet.

But before he can reach the door, Sarah grabs him by the elbow, stopping him in his tracks. 'I'll call you later,' she tells him. He has the grace to throw a glance at me before nodding at my wife and leaving my house.

Sarah rounds on me, her voice filled with exasperation. 'I don't know what the hell is going on with you,' she starts, but as I stand up, looming over her, her words falter under the intensity of my furious glare. She squeaks, 'You're acting weirder than ever, and Georgia really needs you right now.'

'You don't get to tell me what to do,' I spit out, my voice venomous. 'Has it even crossed your thick skull that I'm like this because of *you*? This is all on you, Sarah. You and this pathetic excuse for a marriage.'

'Zack, you have to stop blaming me for whatever mess you've got yourself into. If you're not happy, then just leave. Please just go!'

I stand my ground, my jaw set in stubborn defiance. 'I'm not going anywhere. This is my house. And that girl up there is my daughter.'

A glint flickers across her face that makes me feel sick, but she shakes it away again. 'You want me to leave? Fine. I can get some money together,' Sarah says, a hint of determination creeping into her voice.

Hope dances across my mind. The prospect of finally being free of Sarah is being dangled in front of me and it feels divine. But I know what will happen if she goes. I know I can kiss goodbye to my daughter. The idea of Sarah leaving is ludicrous. I laugh in her face, and she recoils. 'Good luck with that. You have been leeching off me for years, and with the prenup ...'

'Then help me out. I don't want to be here as much as you want me gone. I just need a little head start.'

'That's not happening.'

'Why not? If you help me, I can go, and we can both be happy.'

'Because you'll take her away from me.' I feel ashamed by the whine in my voice, but hell will freeze over before I pay for Sarah to take Georgia away from me.

'I won't, Zack. I promise.'

She's lying. And she isn't stealing my daughter away from me. They're not going anywhere.

CHAPTER 21

I arrive in the office on time but as soon as I take a step over the threshold, Chelsea takes one look at me and shakes her head.

'Don't tell me you're going to see clients looking like that?'

I automatically raise my fingers to touch my top lip. The split in my skin stings at the contact. I know I look terrible. As well as the split lip, my bloodshot left eye is surrounded by a mottled bruise, I have a cut along my knuckles on my right hand, and I look beyond exhausted after not sleeping this last week.

I don't know what to say to Chelsea. Everything is such a mess, and I don't have the words to explain how I feel and what I'm going through.

Chelsea sighs at me and stands. 'That's it. I'm not doing this anymore.'

Alarm shoots through me. 'What are you doing?'

'I cannot work here, Zack. I took this job because I thought you were a man of integrity and professionalism. I thought you lived for helping the victims of monsters, but when I look at you now?' Her pause takes my breath away. 'I don't know who you are anymore, Zack.

And to be honest, I don't want to be here when the shit hits the fan. You don't pay me enough for that.'

Her insult bites at me. I used to feel so much pride in everything I've built. Discharging clients who have successfully built new lives for themselves gave my life purpose. And I still want that, but my life has thrown me so many curveballs lately that I no longer feel that sense of joy I get from helping people.

'Chelsea, please don't go.' My whimper makes her head snap up and away from her desk drawer that she's emptying into her bag. The weight of her gaze makes me slump into a chair. Shamefully, I realise tears are slipping down my cheeks and I bury my face in my hands.

The seat shifts next to me as Chelsea sits down. Her voice is gentle but firm. 'Zack, I don't know what's going on with you, but you need to sort your shit out. You're pushing me and your clients away.'

My sobs come harder. When I sit back and think about my life, I can't fathom how or when things got so messed up. My marriage is in shambles, my wife enjoys putting me through hell. The light brought into my life by Millie has gone. Dad is sick and blaming me for the downward spiral of my marriage. My brother is more messed up than ever and blaming me.

Why is everything my fault? I have tried to be a good man. I have always had the best of intentions. What have I done to deserve all this? It seems that no good deed goes unpunished.

Chelsea waits for my sobbing to subside and gives me a moment to pull myself together.

'I don't want to lose you,' I tell her. If I lose Chelsea, I'll lose the business. She's the only thing holding it all together right now and no one can handle the business like Chelsea.

The anger behind her eyes softens. 'I don't want you to lose me either. But Zack, if you keep on the way you are, you'll have no clients left and the business will fold. There's an admin job going at my dad's construction company. I have to protect myself. I have a wedding to pay for.'

'I will sort this out. It's all family stuff. I can fix this.'

'Family?' she asks with raised eyebrows. 'Not Emily O'Neale?'

I maintain eye contact and pray she'll believe my lie. 'That was a mistake. It'll never happen again.'

'Oh, please. My mum always said, "Once a cheat, always a cheat." You can't expect me to believe you'll never sleep with her again. She's gorgeous, for a start.'

'I have never slept with her!'

'Oh, please ... There's something dodgy going on between you two ...'

'No, really, Chelsea. I have never slept with Millie. It was a kiss, one kiss. There's nothing else between us.'

She pauses to look at me with her calculating gaze. 'Fine,' she says eventually. 'What you did was still so wrong, though. Emily is vulnerable, Zack. You must realise that.'

'I know,' I whisper. 'It was a mistake.'

She pauses, tapping her fingertips on her skirt. She sighs. 'Look, at the end of the day, your personal business is none of mine. But, I helped you grow this business and it means so much to me. I can't just sit here and watch you destroy it all.'

I allow hope to flood my senses. Chelsea won't leave me. She can't. We're a team and she has alway said she'd hate to work at her dad's company. Being surrounded by builders was Chelsea's idea of a nightmare.

She continues with a sad shake of her head. 'But Zack, I absolutely hate cheaters. Consider this my formal notice. And I'm taking today off to see my dad.'

'No, you can't do that.' I clutch her hand, but she pulls it away. 'What if I give you a little bonus to help with your wedding?'

She chuckles. 'You're trying to buy me?'

'It's more of a show of confidence. I *will* pull myself together and get the practice back on track. We'll get back to normal. I just need some time to get my head together, and maybe a lump sum for the wedding will ease your stress levels while you wait for me.'

She stares at the floor, considering my offer. The decision seems to take forever, and I breathe a loud sigh of relief when she finally nods. 'Fine. But if I don't see you getting your act together in the next fortnight, I'm going.'

'I understand,' I tell her. 'I've got this.'

She stands and goes back to her desk where she slowly begins to take stationery out of her bag and carefully put it back in place. 'I'll cancel today's appointments. You can't face people looking like that.'

'Thank you.'

As she takes her seat, she looks up at me, sadness shrouding her. 'Zack, for what it's worth, I like you. I want you to be happy. You've got one life. Don't waste it by throwing it all away.'

She's right, of course. But what she doesn't realise is that Millie and Georgia are the good in my life. And it's time I fought for my girls.

I slip out and leave Chelsea in the office rescheduling this week's appointments. I can't fault that girl's work ethic. My clients love her, and I am utterly grateful to have her in my life, holding things together.

I head along the high street to meet with my solicitor who I persuaded to meet me at short notice. There must be a way I can get full custody of Georgia. Sarah is an alcoholic leech, a stain on Georgia's life. I just need to convince everyone else of that.

CHAPTER 22

'Come in! Dad's in the living room.' Mum ushers us inside. She looks radiant tonight in a floor-length emerald skirt and sequined top.

'You look like a mermaid, Nana!' Georgia exclaims, pushing past me to seek solace from the rain. She's hit the nail on the head – my mum *does* resemble a mythical sea creature.

'Thank you, honey!' Mum ruffles Georgia's hair as she dashes past and vanishes into the living room. 'And how are you doing, Zack?' she asks me, pulling me in for a hug. She's lost weight. I can feel her ribs through her top and her face looks drawn.

'Yeah, I'm fine,' I lie. I'm in a foul mood and the source of my misery strolls in behind me.

'Hi, Theresa! Long time no see. How are you?' Sarah asks Mum, shaking off her umbrella onto the doorstep.

Mum turns away from me and puts an arm around my wife. They launch into a conversation about Mum's latest book club gossip, completely forgetting about me. I leave them chatting in the hallway, unable to wipe the scowl from my face.

I find my father sitting in the armchair by the fire, a blanket on his knee. Georgia is perched on the arm of his chair, telling him about the present I bought him for his birthday. I roll my eyes as she gives away the surprise.

'Georgia here tells me you got me some "mega" expensive whiskey!' Dad calls out to me.

I laugh, feeling some of my bad mood evaporate. 'So much for it being a secret,' I say, tousling Georgia's hair.

'This is just a little secret, Daddy. I'm good at keeping big secrets.' She looks at me with wide eyes, the reproach boring a hole into my conscience. I couldn't give a damn about lying to Sarah, but burdening my little girl with the secret of my infidelity weighs heavily on my shoulders.

'Well, crack it open then, son.' My dad gestures at his empty glass. Mum and Sarah flit past as they head to the kitchen. The smell of garlic, tomato sauce, and Mum's floral perfume wafts behind them – a scent that transports me back to my childhood.

'You're looking well, Dad. Feeling better?' I pour us each a shot of whiskey and hand one to Dad before taking a seat on the sofa.

'Of course! You can't keep an old boy like me down for long.' We clink our glasses and savour the golden liquid. I relish the burn as it slides down my throat.

'How many years is it now, Dad? Ninety-two?'

Dad barks out a laugh. 'Cheeky bastard! I'm seventy-two.'

'Pops!' Georgia admonishes. 'Swearing is naughty.'

'That's very true. Now, why don't you go and help the women in the kitchen?'

Georgia tuts at him theatrically before hopping off the chair. 'That's *sexism*, Pops.' But she runs off into the kitchen anyway, where she's greeted with a high-pitched chorus.

'You heard from Aaron?' I ask to fill the silence Georgia's left behind.

'No. He'll be here, though.' Dad sounds confident, but I'm doubtful. Aaron has a knack for letting people down. Just ask the army. 'Mum made him promise and you know how that boy dotes on her. A proper mummy's boy.'

I still feel doubtful. For the last year, my brother has barely been around. He chooses to spend his time pretending not to exist and hiding from the world. His connection with Mum is diminishing by the day and it crushes me to think of how that must make her feel. Aaron was always Mum's golden boy, but now he's barely there.

I haven't given much thought to his appearances at mine, but now I wonder what it is he really wanted. He's never been close to Dad, and he's pulling away from Mum. So why come to me? What is it he wants?

'Dinner's ready,' Sarah says, peering around the door. Her cheeks are already flushed from the wine.

Dad goes to lift himself out of his chair, but his arms fail him, and he slumps back down. Despite looking a little better, his weeks of illness have left him frail and weakened. I grasp an elbow and pull Dad up, and he leans on me so I can help him to the dining room. 'Thanks, lad. I need to get back to the gym.'

Is this why Mum has lost so much weight? Has she been carting Dad around? What kind of life are they living here? I'm angry at myself for being distracted by Millie and not noticing Dad's deterioration. But I am furious at Dad for being so damn stubborn about seeing a doctor.

Millie has been quite the distraction, though. Missing her these last few weeks has driven me insane and to get my fix I have joined her gym and discovered a dance studio that offers a great vantage point of the entire gym floor – the perfect spot from which to watch her. If she won't contact me, I have to check on her in other ways.

I need to let go of my fear of what happened at her house the last time we met. The more time that slips by, the more convinced I am that I never touched Dexter. And Millie has never looked better. No bruising, a brighter smile, a spring in her step.

It's time we resumed our relationship. It's time I paid her a real visit.

We all take our seats at the table. Bowls of buttered vegetables and various types of pasta dishes stretch out before me. An Italian feast. Sarah takes the seat opposite me, with Georgia on her right. Sarah's glass is nearly empty, and her teeth are already stained red.

'I'd like to make a quick toast before we dig in,' Dad says, not bothering to stand.

'Shouldn't we wait for Aaron?' Mum asks, her eyes not leaving the empty chair to my left.

'No,' Dad says bluntly. 'Dinner will go cold. It's not our fault he's off gallivanting.'

As if on cue, the front door slams shut and we all spin to watch the door. Only the sound of Sarah tapping on the tablecloth breaks the silence. I resist the urge to scowl at her.

Aaron walks in hesitantly and recoils when he sees us all staring at him. 'Alright?' he asks.

I scoff.

'Nice of you to turn up!' Dad says. He hates tardiness. Punctuality is a sign of respect for my father and if you lose his respect, it takes a hell of a long time to earn it back. Although I suspect Dad's respect for Aaron is long gone. I could never work out why, and I have given up trying.

'Come and sit down, Aaron. It's great to see you, darling,' says Mum, ever the diplomatic one.

He walks over to the empty seat next to me and pulls out the chair. It scrapes noisily against the floor, making Georgia giggle. 'Sounded like a fart,' she snorts.

The tension breaks, and we all burst out laughing. Even my brother manages a grin.

'Are you going to tell us why you're late?' Dad asks my brother once we're all settled and the food has been served. 'Or are you just going to waltz in here like it doesn't matter?'

Aaron shovels a forkful of carbonara into his mouth like he hasn't eaten in months. His shirt is creased, and there's a small rip on the thigh of his jeans. He really needs a woman in his life to sort him out. If only there was someone foolish enough to take him on. I look at my wife, deep in conversation with Georgia. She's living proof that there are foolish women out there. The irony that I'm married to her is not lost on me.

'I just got caught up with something,' Aaron tells my dad.

I fight the urge to delve deeper into his poor excuse. But thankfully, Dad isn't done yet. 'Caught up with what?' he asks. 'Finding a girl-friend I hope?'

'Graham,' Mum warns from the other side of the table.

'No, no. It's my birthday, Theresa. I deserve an explanation. He's a big boy. He can handle it.'

Aaron swallows, and I'm shocked to see tears well up in his dark eyes. 'No girlfriend, Dad. Things are just a bit difficult right now, that's all.'

Dad scoffs, and the entire party turns to look at the two of them, each watching the conversation with varying shades of embarrassment on their faces. 'Don't you think it's about time you pulled yourself out of this *depression*? You've been wallowing for far too long, and it's time you became a man. And move forward.'

I swallow, taken aback by my father's frankness. But, let's face it, he's only said what we're all thinking. I can't be the only one sick of my brother's self-pity and moping.

'Dad ...' Aaron stutters. 'It's not that easy.' I turn away, unable to handle my brother's cringeworthy emotions.

Mum stands and slams her palm against the table. 'Right! Now that's enough, Graham.' She points a finger at Dad. 'Stop berating him. He's done nothing wrong.'

'He's done everything wrong!' my dad yells back.

Aaron stands up, his eyes boring into Dad. Then, without a backwards glance, he leaves the house. I can't help but feel a little bit relieved. This party is better off without his presence bringing us down.

Mum and Dad continue to glare at each other. 'Now look what you did,' she says, sitting back down. Her eyes keep flitting to the door, no doubt hoping Aaron will grow some balls and come back to face us.

'Now, Theresa. You have worked hard on this meal. I won't let him ruin it.'

Mum opens her mouth like she's got more to say on the subject but snaps it shut again, not willing to fall out with Dad. In their forty years of marriage, they have never fallen out. This is an alien experience, and I feel deeply uncomfortable.

We all go back to eating, but I notice everyone is just moving food around their plates, appetites lost in the tense atmosphere.

Sarah finishes her glass of wine and reaches for the bottle. 'You know, Aaron could really use his family right now,' she declares, out of the blue.

I snap. 'Shut up, Sarah. This is a family matter. It has nothing to do with you.'

Georgia drops her fork with a clatter. Sarah pauses, the bottle of wine tilted and hovering over her glass.

'Zack, don't be so nasty,' Mum warns.

Her reprimand only serves to deepen my anger. How dare she have Sarah's side? Can Mum really not see what is happening here? Sarah has no right to defend my brother. Whatever Aaron has done, Dad's treatment of him is justified. Dad would never treat someone with disdain if they didn't deserve it.

'How dare you talk to me about family,' Sarah spits at me. 'You don't know one thing about family values.'

'You've had too much to drink. Maybe go and get some air?' I waft my hand at her, treating her like the child she's behaving like.

All eyes are on us now, the entertainment. I daren't look at Georgia in case guilt makes me lose my resolve with Sarah.

'Maybe you should be the one to get some air,' Sarah slurs back. She goes to pour the wine but misses, pouring wine over the white tablecloth.

I snap again. 'For fuck's sake, Sarah! You're a disgrace.' My voice is far louder than I intended, but the volume feels good. It fits my mood. 'You shouldn't even be here. You're not welcome in this family! You're a shit wife and a shit mum!'

'Daddy!' Georgia screeches. I'm horrified to see her eyes wide open, her mouth skewed in terror, and her skin flushed with anxiety.

'It's okay, honey. It's just grown-ups talking. We're sorting things out,' I tell her, reaching over to touch her hand.

'Don't lie to me, Daddy. No more lies!' She pulls her hand away from mine, her little face glowing with rage.

My jaw tenses. 'It's okay, Georgie. Everything is okay.'

'But it isn't, is it?! It hasn't been okay for a long time. That's why you were having sex with that lady!'

The tension in the room is thick enough to cut with a knife. I refuse to make eye contact with my parents. I'm mortified that my father had to find out like this.

Out of the corner of my eye, I see Sarah lean back in her chair and shove a forkful of food in her mouth.

'Zack?' Mum gasps. 'How could you?'

My mouth bobs open, but Sarah beats me to it. 'Oh, don't worry, Theresa. I already knew about his dirty little secret.'

Now my eyes snap up to hers. She meets my gaze and slams her fork down on her plate. 'What I didn't know,' she continues, still chewing on pasta, 'is that our six-year-old girl knew about it, too. Did you seriously think it was okay to ask her to keep your dirty little secret? How could you do that to her, Zack?'

My eyes flit between my daughter and my wife.

'I think we should give you some space,' Mum announces, making a move to leave.

'No!' Sarah barks, stopping Mum in her tracks. 'You shouldn't have to leave your own table. We're all family here and Zack should be honest with us. For once in his life.'

'How did you find out?' I ask her. 'Georgia, did you ...?'

'Don't you dare blame her!' Sarah snaps. 'I didn't even know she was aware. How did she find out, Zack?'

I swallow. 'That doesn't matter. So, if it wasn't Georgia, how *did* you find out?'

Sarah sneers at me. 'Your receptionist called me. Apparently, she believes in the sanctity of marriage and couldn't stand to keep it to herself.'

Fucking Chelsea.

I run my hand through my hair and blow out a breath. This can't be happening. Sarah has no right to humiliate me like this.

'Right, that's enough,' I announce. 'We're not doing this here.'

'We'll do this where I damn well please. I have been nothing but honest with you, and the whole time you have been sleeping with someone behind my back.' She throws a glance at Georgia, whose eyes widen in shock. Sarah drops her voice to a soothing tone. 'How did you find out, honey?'

'I saw them,' Georgia mumbles, her eyes fixed on the table. 'In his office.'

My dad groans into his hand. Mum gasps. I squeeze my eyes shut and press my hands over them.

'You slept with her while our daughter was there?'

'I haven't slept with her!' I yell. I need them all to know I didn't take it that far.

'For Christ's sake, Zack. What the hell is wrong with you? You're a fucking mess.'

'Don't you *dare* disrespect me like that!'

'Now stop!' Dad yells, supporting himself on the table and pushing himself into a standing position. 'Pull yourselves together. Both of you. This is no way to behave around a child.'

A brief silence settles over us before Sarah pushes her chair out. 'Come on, Georgia. We're going home.'

'You can't drive in that state,' I tell her. 'You're hammered.'

'I'm not stupid, Zack. I'll call a cab. And I'm certainly not hammered. Why do you always exaggerate how much I drink?'

'You should wait inside, darling. It's raining out there,' Mum tells her.

'I can't, Theresa. I can't be in this house with *that* man.' Sarah ushers Georgia out of the dining room and we sit and listen to them put on their shoes and coats.

The food on my plate in front of me gives off a noxious smell, making me feel sick.

When the front door slams shut behind my wife and daughter, Dad speaks up. 'Can I have a moment alone with my son?'

Mum hesitates, not wanting to leave us alone. 'Now, Theresa!' Dad shouts.

Mum throws me a look of disappointment laced with concern before vacating the dining room.

It's not until we have the room to ourselves that Dad sits back down heavily into his chair. I wait as he arranges his cutlery neatly on his plate. I feel like a naughty schoolboy waiting for my detention. 'Dad ...' I venture, but he raises his hand at me.

'We talked about this last time,' he says. 'You promised it wouldn't happen again.'

I shake my head. 'Dad, this isn't the same. I haven't slept with her.'

'But you're having an affair? You have feelings for this girl?'

'Yes. Dad, I love her.' There's no point in lying. Not when everything is so exposed anyway.

He laughs heartily like I have just told him the world's best joke. '*Love*? Son, I don't think you know the meaning of the word.'

'Of course I do. Millie is different. She's special. You'll like her.'

'How can I like the woman you've used to hurt your wife? Stop talking shit. You made a promise to me that you will fix your marriage. And after what happened last time, I figured you'd be a fool to go against your word.'

I swallow. Last time was different. How I felt about Katie was different. I thought I had strong feelings for her – but I was wrong.

'Millie,' Dad mumbles.

'What?'

'You said her name is Millie.' He speaks her name with such venom it makes me recoil.

'Dad. Please. Millie is a good girl. She's good for me.'

'So's your wife!' I sink into my seat. 'I have told you over and over the importance of marriage. Keeping the spark alive is your responsibility. You can't take it for granted, and you can't just go looking for it elsewhere. It's immoral.'

'That's just it, Dad. There was never a spark there to begin with.'

'But you married her, Zack! You made a promise. A *vow*. And you've gone against your word. You're a disgrace to the family.'

'You don't know everything about Sarah.'

'Don't fool yourself. I know everything. *Nothing* slips past me unnoticed.'

I hang my head in shame. Though I cannot summon regret.

I'll work things out with Millie. I'll show them all.

CHAPTER 23

The moon is high in the sky when I eventually make it home. Whiskey runs through my veins, an inadequate tonic to kill my pain.

I press the door closed quietly behind me. I don't intend to stay long. Then I'll come back tomorrow for Georgia. Screw what the solicitor said. I don't need some overpaid pompous idiot in an expensive suit telling me what I can and can't do with my daughter.

I'm shoving shirts into a suit-carrier when Sarah enters my room. 'Leaving without saying goodbye?' Her voice is obnoxiously loud.

'Shh, you'll wake Georgia.' That's if she's even sleeping. After tonight's shitshow, she'll probably be awake all night.

'You don't need to worry about that.'

I stop in my tracks, my back tense. I can hear the smirk in her voice, and I desperately don't want to play her game, but I take the bait anyway. 'What do you mean?'

'You just don't need to concern yourself with Georgia. She isn't here.'

'Where is she?' I growl.

'No need to sound so aggressive, Zack. She's at my sister's. I figured you'd come home in a foul mood, and I didn't think it would be good for her to be here for it.'

'I'm done with this. Done with you. I'm going to get my daughter and go. I'm leaving you.'

She raises an eyebrow at me. '*Your* daughter, Zack?'

She's winding me up. Of course Georgia is mine. How dare she insinuate otherwise? Fury tears through me. 'Get the fuck out of here, Sarah. Before I do something I regret.'

'Your whole life is a massive regret, isn't it? I mean, just being *you* must be hard to live with. You're pathetic. Always looking in all the wrong places to make your life better when the problem is *you*.'

My teeth grind together as I take a step towards her. She doesn't flinch. 'You're just a disgusting drunk. I will not let you get to me,' I spit at her.

'We both know that's not true, Zack. I know what you've been telling people – how I'm always drinking, how I'm an unfit mother. Yet we both know that's a load of bollocks. You exaggerate in the pathetic hope you'll get full custody of Georgia. Well, I hate to break it to you, but it's not going to work. There's no way in hell you'll get any access to my little girl.'

'You will not take her away from me!' I roar. I jab my finger into her chest, forcing her to stumble back onto the landing. 'She is *my* girl.'

Sarah laughs at me. The cackle comes with a deep sense of truth and the fear that rips through me is unbearable. 'Sorry Zack, but that's just not true. Georgia isn't yours.'

It's as if all of my senses have shut off. I can only see a blinding white light, and my ears are ringing with static. I feel my arms reach out in front of me, and I lunge forward. Her body feels soft beneath the palms of my hands, and I have to push hard to shove her heavy weight. I feel her give way beneath the force of my push.

I regain my senses just as Sarah lands at the bottom of the stairs. There's a sickening crack as she hits the wall at the bottom. Streetlight pouring in through the door illuminates a smear of blood down the wallpaper. I drop my arms to my sides with a deep sense of satisfaction.

I can't see her breathing.

A smile spreads across my face as I look down at her motionless body.

As I wait in vain to see Sarah move, a delirious panic takes over and my laughter rings out in the dark. My twisted joy steals my breath, and I have to take a seat on the top stair until I can calm down and think straight.

Sarah, the weight on my shoulders, the pain in my arse, is gone. After years of plotting how I can leave her without losing custody of my daughter, I have finally been given a way out.

I head back into my room, where I carefully place the clothing I've packed back into my wardrobe.

Heading downstairs, I step over Sarah, resisting the urge to spit on her as I pass. 'Bye, bitch,' I sneer. 'That's what you get for lying about *my* daughter.'

CHAPTER 24

M illie's bedroom light is on when I pull up outside her house. I cast my mind back to my first visit here, back when I pleasured myself outside. Oh, how things have changed.

Now Sarah is gone, I no longer have to suffer my secret obsession. I am free to claim my prize and raise *my* daughter with Millie. Without Sarah tainting everything with her lies and menace.

I am regaining control of my life. The path is clearing and everything feels somewhat easier now. I can do anything. I can have everything. And nothing can stop me. The stars twinkle down at me, blessing me with a promising future. I feel light on my feet, and I practically skip to Millie's front door.

I rap on the door with a jaunty beat. A fresh wind sweeps past me, making me shiver.

No answer.

I knock again, harder this time, in case Millie is asleep and can't hear me. Once she hears me out, she won't mind. Once she knows I am here to claim her and give her the life she deserves.

Finally, I see movement behind the door and the hall light switches on. Her petite figure gets larger as she moves closer to the door.

'Zack?' she gasps when she pulls the door open. Her hair is mussed up around her face and her cheeks are flushed. I tingle at the thought of what lies beneath her fluffy dressing gown. What it'll feel like to run my hands over the soft skin. 'What's wrong? You look ... insane.'

'Sorry to interrupt your evening.' I wring my hands together. 'I didn't know where else to go.'

'Why are you here? What's going on?'

'Sarah knows about us. And the bitch told my entire family, so I came straight here from Dad's.' I pause, letting the lie settle in. 'And with Dexter gone ...'

'Us? Zack, you must know there is no *us*. I thought we were done. After what happened last time we were together ...'

'I just need somewhere to stay tonight. Then tomorrow, I'll get everything sorted, and you can finally leave this place. We can be together.' I can hear the desperate madness in my voice and I swallow it back.

'Zack, I ...' Her confusion adds to her cuteness.

I place my hands on her shoulders and bring my face close to hers, but she pulls away before I can kiss her.

'Look, Zack, I'm sorry if I gave you the wrong impression. I thought I put things straight. I haven't spoken to you in weeks!'

I cock my head to the side and give her my practised sorrowful look I reserve for clients. 'It's okay to feel afraid, Millie. You've been through so much. And you have so many unanswered questions, but I'm offering you a way out. Move in with me and we'll take this at your pace. Then when you're ready, we can put a label on our relationship. No pressure.'

'No, Zack! What is wrong with you?' Her tone is harsh. I've come on too strong, and she's pulling away. I imagine this is quite a lot to take in.

I take a deep breath, trying to push away my frustration and adopt a gentler approach. 'You don't have to be scared anymore. I will never hurt you. Millie, I'm in love with you. You hear me? I love you.'

'Millie?' The deep, husky voice comes from upstairs.

'I'll be there in a sec,' she calls back, glaring at me. She pushes the door and I jam my foot in the doorway to stop it from closing.

'Is that Dexter?' I ask her, keeping my voice low in case the bastard is listening. 'Millie, don't let him trap you again. Leave with me, right now. I can protect you. You don't have to live like this.'

She reaches through the gap in the door and grazes the back of her hand over my cheek. The pity in her eyes ignites a storm inside of me. 'I'm sorry, Zack. I'm so sorry. You've got to go. And don't come back. It's for your own good.'

'Don't do this. Don't take him back. You were doing so well.'

'I *am* doing so well, Zack. For your information, that isn't Dexter upstairs.'

I feel like the Earth has opened up and swallowed me whole. Millie has moved on with someone else. Not with me.

'Who's up there?' I scowl, elbowing the door open wider and stepping into the warm hallway.

She pulls me back. 'Don't you dare go up there! Who I'm sleeping with has nothing to do with you. You were my therapist, Zack. Not my boyfriend. And, from now on, you're nothing to me.'

'Please, Millie,' I plead. I rest my hands on her cheeks, but she pushes them away and takes my hands in hers.

Her tone is soft like she's talking to an over-emotional child. 'Zack, I'm so sorry if you got the wrong impression. I was healing and you were there for me. Maybe I made some errors in judgement and got too involved with you, but I didn't think *you* would be the one to take it so far. You're supposed to be the professional.' She sighs and lets go of my hands.

'But I am a professional, Millie. I know exactly what's best for you. We would be so good together ...'

'You need to leave.'

The stranger calls out once more. 'Mills, everything all right down there?'

'Millie ...' I whisper.

'Yeah, it's fine. I've got this.'

'Millie, please ...'

'Get out, Zack,' she says through gritted teeth, but I refuse to move. 'Get out!'

'You can't do this!' I raise my voice now. Sod the man upstairs. Sod the slag standing in front of me. 'You can't just push me away!'

'Watch me.' With surprising strength, she pushes me out the door. I trip over the threshold, smashing my coccyx on the path. The impact ricochets up my spine and I cry out in pain.

When I glance back up at the house, Millie is gone.

CHAPTER 25

I spend the rest of the night driving around aimlessly. Seething.

Millie isn't thinking clearly. That much is obvious. She's so fragile and broken from Dexter's abuse, it's no wonder she's flailing around, badly trying to piece herself back together. I just need to make her see sense and draw her back to me.

My anger lies purely with the man in her bed. The thought of his hands on her bare skin, breathing in her feminine scent, taking her, defiling her. I roar, slamming my palms against the steering wheel.

Everything is spinning out of control. How have I let the possibility of happiness slip through my fingers? And most crucially, how can I turn this around and live the life I deserve?

Every now and then, Sarah invades my thoughts. Her mangled body lying at the foot of the stairs. Her blood splashed on the wall, ruining the wallpaper. As much a mess in death as in life.

I need to deal with her body before Georgia gets home. I can't let my little girl be the one to discover her like that. It would destroy her, and she doesn't deserve that.

As the sun first peeks over the horizon, I begin to regain my composure. Millie is the ultimate prize, so of course she's a challenge to win. And I'm more than willing to fight for her. This is a minor setback, nothing more.

And I have to focus on the positives here. Sarah is gone, taken care of. Everyone will just think this was a tragic accident brought on by a dependence on booze and a tendency to be clumsy.

Now I just have to drop her body into the ground, and I can live happily ever after with Georgia. And I will be ready with open arms when Millie feels able to complete our family.

A smile plays across my face as I pull up outside my home. I have a plan. First, I just have to clean up the mess in the house and then I can wipe the slate clean. All is not lost.

I slide my key into the lock, but I'm surprised to feel no resistance when I try to turn it. The door is unlocked.

I locked it, didn't I? Yes, I distinctly remember doing so, as Sarah would have done when she got home last night. Before tragically tumbling down the stairs in a drunken stupor.

I push open the door with ludicrous slowness, as if Sarah's corpse might jump out and startle me as a punishment for pushing her. I can't shake the sick feeling as I step into the house with trepidation. My hand trails along the wall as I round the corner to where I left my wife crumpled in the hall.

She's not there.

Her blood remains on the wall and a small red stain has spread over the carpet.

The events of last night aren't a delusion. I run my hand through my hair, gasping for breath. What happened to her?

'No, no, no,' I mutter to myself, imagining Georgia coming home to find her mum's body. Could I have fucked up that badly?

No, it's barely six a.m. There's no way Sarah's sister would have dropped Georgia back this early in the morning. Helen is a stay-at-home mum, I doubt she's ever seen that early in the day. Plus, surely if a body had been discovered, there'd be more commotion. A police presence.

Did Sarah survive the fall and wander off? I realise for the first time that in the midst of my madness, I never checked her pulse. I heard the crack of a bone breaking, saw blood, and assumed. Assumption is clearly the mother of all fuck-ups.

Even if Sarah survived, there's no way she could have just gotten up and walked away. She was broken. But, to my horror, still able to tell the truth about what really happened last night – how this was all my fault.

'Damn it!' I shout. Terror forcing me into action, I race through the house, calling her name. I check the bedrooms to see if she's gone for a lie-down. I check the kitchen, hoping to see her sitting there, nursing a cup of tea. Or a glass of wine. I even check the garden in case she's getting some fresh air.

She's not here.

I pace around the living room, trying to decide my next move. I need to think of a game plan that won't land me in trouble and to do that, I need answers before Georgia gets home. I have no idea when that will be, and the clock is ticking.

The best thing to do is to call Helen and delay Georgia's return to buy myself some time to figure things out. I go to pull my phone out of my back pocket, but it's not there. I rush back to my car to find it lying on the passenger seat where I left it, on silent mode. I haven't given it a second's thought since Millie ripped my heart out.

Six missed calls. All from Helen. *Shit.*

I call her back with trembling hands, and she picks up on the first ring. 'Zack!'

'Helen, what's happened?' I am terrified for my little girl and what she might have seen. I can barely catch my breath as I wait for Helen to respond.

'Where the fuck have you been?' Wow, vulgar, just like her sister. 'You sicken me, you piece of shit.'

She knows. She knows I pushed Sarah down the stairs. My heart stops beating. I toy with the idea of hanging up and running, but my mouth just bobs open instead, searching for the words to get me out of this mess.

'You cheated on her?'

And there it is – my get-out-of-jail-free card. Helen doesn't know what I did.

I ignore her accusation. This has nothing to do with her. 'Helen, do you know where Sarah is?'

A sob catches in her throat, stunning me. Helen is one of those women who never shows weakness. Ever since their dad walked out on them when they were small, and their mum was riddled with cancer, Helen took it upon herself to take care of the family. She was the protector and there was never any room for anything but strength and resilience. Strong and admirable, yes; but she's also fucking annoying.

'She's in hospital. Zack, she fell down the stairs and cracked her skull open. They're operating on her now.'

She doesn't mention me. There's no blame there. No hint of accusation. 'Where's Georgia?'

'She's here at the hospital. I tried to get her to come back to mine, but she didn't want to leave her mum. I don't think she should be here in case, you know ... In case we get bad news.'

I hang up the phone and charge out of the driveway, my foot slamming down hard on the accelerator.

***

I find Helen perched on the edge of a plastic blue chair, as if ready to bolt.

'Where is she?' I ask.

She looks at me with undisguised fury. 'She's still in surgery.'

'Not her. Georgia. Where is she?'

She clenches her jaw. 'There's a kids' room around the corner. She's in there reading a book.'

'You left her on her own?' I turn to leave but Helen stands, halting me in my tracks.

'Of course I didn't. She's with Daniel.'

Daniel is Helen's fourteen-year-old son. Despite Helen being a fucking nightmare, I have to admit she's done right by that boy. He's polite and well-mannered and I trust him with Georgia completely. Miracles do happen.

'Were you with your little whore last night?' Helen scowls at me. 'When your wife lay dying, were you out shagging your little plaything?'

I wince. 'Don't be so crude, Helen. Millie isn't my plaything. And I wasn't with her. How do you know about that anyway?'

'Georgia told me. Whilst bawling her eyes out last night. She was so upset and needed her Hugsy bear, so I offered to take her home to fetch it. She needed it to help her calm down. She insisted on coming with me.' Helen approaches me with her chest jutted out. For a second, I think she's going to punch me. 'That girl deserves so much better than you. You put her through unbelievable pressure and then she had to face her mum like that. She's been through far too much for her age.'

My worst nightmare has been realised. 'Georgia saw her lying there? She saw Sarah in that state?'

Helen sighs and shakes her head. She sits back down, a broken woman. 'No,' she sighs. 'I was worried you two would be fighting, so I left her in the car. She saw nothing.'

I collapse into the chair opposite Helen's. I'm in the clear. Georgia didn't discover her mum left for dead. And no one knows I am responsible. My only fear now is that Sarah wakes up and reveals the truth.

There's always something to deal with. I'm just so tired. I rest my head in my hands and close my eyes whilst Helen breathes deeply in front of me.

'Daddy?' Georgia's voice drifts over, so soft and sweet. She's standing in front of me, her eyes wide with concern. 'It's going to be okay, Daddy. The doctor said so.' She presses her tiny hands on my cheeks and squeezes.

I take her hands in mine and kiss her forehead. I breathe in her citrus-scented shampoo. 'I know, baby. You're okay. Everything will be fine.'

She clambers onto my lap, tucks her head into my chest and immediately falls asleep.

Everything will be fine.

CHAPTER 26

The doctor utters the words I've been dreading: 'Your wife is awake.' It's like a bomb has gone off in my head. 'She is in the High Dependency Unit, where she's getting the very best care.'

It's the moment of truth. Is Sarah going to destroy my life?

A cold chill runs down my body as I lock eyes with him, trying to see behind his eyes. Has Sarah already told him what I did? Has he called the police?

'How is she?' I stutter.

'Groggy, but that's to be expected after what she's been through. Her cognitive function appears okay, but only time will tell.'

He drones on about the impact of a bleed on the brain, but my mind is elsewhere. Shit. I had been praying her memory had been wiped clean. If her cognitive function is okay, then she must remember everything. I am praying for a damn miracle.

Thankfully, Helen took Georgia and Daniel back to hers for a break an hour ago. Georgia was so tired it upset her stomach, and I thought it best she slept in a proper bed, not just curled up in my arms. Now I can get to Sarah before Georgia does. I need to face the music alone.

I chew on my nails as I step into her room. The blinds are closed, casting strips of light across Sarah's face. She looks pale and limp – like death. I take a seat next to the bed and watch as my wife drifts in and out of consciousness, oblivious to my presence. Tubes exit her skull, draining fluids from underneath layers of bandages.

There's a clatter in the corner of the room, making me jump. I spin around to find a nurse bustling about, placing a blood pressure monitor on a trolley and making notes on a tiny strip of paper. I silently will her to finish quickly and leave.

Sarah groans and reaches out for the water on the bedside table. The nurse goes to fetch it for her. 'No need. I can do it,' I tell her. The nurse gives me a pitiful smile before leaving the room.

I take the beaker and place it in Sarah's hands, wrapping her fingers around it to help her grasp it. I bring the straw to her lips but she gags as soon as the water touches her tongue. I reach out and take the drink away before she spills it on the covers.

We sit in silence. She hasn't yet opened her eyes, but I know she knows who's sitting by her side. I can see the tension in her body. My mere presence puts her on edge and that doesn't bode well. I wait for her to speak first. I need to know what she has to say for herself before I jump in with assumptions.

'Zack,' she says finally. 'Are you there?' Her voice is gentle. Weak. The usual fire in her tone isn't there and hope flirts with me.

'I'm here.'

Her fingers twitch in a feeble wiggle in my direction. I take her hand in mine.

'Can I get you anything?' I ask her. It isn't the question I want to ask, but I need to bide my time. I need to be nice and play by her rules.

'No,' she croaks. Her words take an age to form on her lips and my impatience is driving me insane. 'I didn't think you'd come here.'

'Of course I came. You're still my wife, despite everything.' I watch her face carefully, searching for signs of what she remembers.

And there it is – her lips press together like she's deciding how to phrase what she has to say next. My pulse races. I send out a silent prayer. Please God, be on *my* side for once. I'm not a religious man, but it's worth a shot – it's all I have left.

'Zack, what happened last night ...' She slowly brings her free hand to her chest, where I pushed her. 'I'm sorry I told your family about your affair. It was undignified and unfair. I should have spoken to you first. Spared everyone the embarrassment.'

I try to speak, but no words come out. What is happening here?

She continues. 'Let's face it, our marriage has always been a sham. I shouldn't have been surprised you're looking elsewhere. But your parents didn't deserve to find out like that. Especially on your dad's birthday. And as for poor Georgia ...'

Why is she being so amicable? 'Sarah, I'm so sorry you had to find out the way you did.'

She waves away my apology. 'All this,' she says as she gestures at her head, 'has made me see sense. We can't keep doing this to each other. We need to find a way to separate without punishing each other. Life is just too short. You're a good dad to Georgia, I'd never deprive you of seeing her. It wouldn't be fair on either of you.'

I long to jump up and release a celebratory scream. All is not lost. She has no idea what happened last night. How I almost killed her and left her there for dead. Feeling bolder, I double-check. 'Sarah, what happened? How did you fall?'

Confusion flits over her bruised features; the movement looks painful. 'I don't know,' she whispers, a tear spilling down her cheek. 'I remember the taxi dropping Georgia off at Helen's. Then when I got home, I opened a bottle of wine. I'm assuming I finished it and tripped down the stairs, but I can't remember.'

I raise my eyes to the heavens, thanking God for having my back at long last.

Sarah stares at the wall in front of her, quietly weeping, and I almost feel sorry for her. She's right about one thing – it's time we ended our marriage. We need to discuss our next move like adults, not like two enemies trying to shoot the fatal shot.

I'm tired of fighting. And I have to conserve my energy to get Millie back. I can have everything I want now, I just need to keep Sarah sweet. For now, at least.

There's a tap on the door, and Mum and Dad wander in, Mum clutching a huge bouquet of chrysanthemums. 'We're not interrupting anything, are we?' Dad asks, pointedly looking at my hand, still clasped around Sarah's. He beams at me, pleased at the affectionate gesture. I let go.

Dad is hell-bent on the sanctity of marriage. If I am honest with myself, that's why I am in this mess. I have always wanted to please Dad, and he's so fixated on Sarah and I being together that breaking up always felt like an impossible choice. How am I going to tell him we've just decided to break up?

Sarah wipes her face on the back of her hand and gestures at the chairs on the other side of her bed. 'Thanks for coming. How did you know I was here?'

'That daughter of yours has been calling everyone she can think of,' Mum chuckles, though it's tinged with concern. 'Telling us about her brave mummy who broke her head open.'

Sarah tuts, but smiles at our daughter's love of gossip.

'So how are you doing, darling?' my dad asks. He takes the flowers from Mum and sets them down on the bedside table. He takes the seat next to Mum, pulling it closer to her. I wonder how he got the flowers in here – I'm pretty sure they aren't allowed in the HDU.

'I've been better,' Sarah admits.

'Really?! But you look like a million dollars!'

'Dad,' I start. This is no time for jokes.

But Sarah just laughs. 'Always playing the comedy card aren't you, Graham?'

'Why do you think Theresa is still with me? It's hardly for my stunning looks.'

Mum pushes Dad on the shoulder, her eyes rolling back affectionately. Their love makes me feel uncomfortable. It's like the more affectionate they are, the more exposed I feel. It's as if they're shining a light on the lack of love between Sarah and I. I know Sarah is feeling it too as she shifts in her slouched position.

'So, what happened to you, you poor thing?' Mum asks, jolting me back to the conversation.

Sarah gulps and turns away. 'I fell down the stairs. I guess I'd had a little too much to drink and tripped.' Her cheeks blush through the bruising.

Mum makes cringeworthy fawning noises, but Dad doesn't react. He simply nods and looks at me. 'And where were you?'

'Driving around,' I shrug. 'I just needed some time alone. Last night was a little tough. On all of us.'

'You're right there,' Dad says, patting Sarah's arm. 'Just as long as you're on the mend, darling?'

'Oh, yes,' Sarah nods. 'I have a fractured skull, but they've patched it back up and given me pain meds for the headaches. The doctor said it'll take some months to fully recover, and there's a chance I'll get headaches for much longer, but I'm alive. That's the main thing.'

'You're solid as a rock. Nothing can keep you down,' Dad chuckles. 'Right, I need a cup of coffee. Zack, will you come and show me where the machine is, please?'

'Sure,' I say, even though I'm confident Dad saw it on the way in here. You can't miss it. 'Can we get you anything?' I ask Mum.

She nods. 'Tea please.'

Sarah says, 'No, thank you.' Despite never being asked.

Dad leads the way down the corridor, straight to the coffee machine situated right by the entrance to the ward. 'What I saw in there ... when we walked in ...' he begins, but I throw my hands up to stop him.

'Dad, I know what it looked like, but I have to be straight with you.' I have to be brave and tell the truth. The lies are building up and I need to get some out of me to relieve the pressure.

Dad taps the machine with his bank card and the machine whirs to life, presenting him a cup. Brown liquid sloshes into the plastic. For the first time I notice how slouched he is. 'Sarah and I have decided to separate.'

He grabs the cup and pulls it to his chest. Squeezing it too tightly, hot black liquid washes over his hand and drips onto the floor. He doesn't seem to notice. 'No. That's not happening.' His voice is a low grumble I can hardly hear. He refuses to meet my eye.

Goosebumps erupt all over my body. I don't think I have defied my dad before. But I can't carry on like this. No one is happy. At least if we split up, there's a chance we can find happiness apart.

'Sorry, Dad. This is best for all of us. Sarah agrees.'

'Sarah doesn't know what she's talking about! Have you seen the state of her? She'd tell you the sky is green right now. She's in no fit state to make such a big decision.'

'That's just it. I think we decided a long time ago. We just didn't have the courage to admit it to one another.'

'That's bullshit!' Dad yells, alerting the attention of the security guard standing by the nurses' station.

'Is everything all right here?' he asks, strolling over. He's inches shorter than my dad and a waif in comparison. Good luck to the guy – he hasn't got a chance.

'It's all fine, mate. Just a little disagreement with my son. I'm sure you understand.' Dad grins at him, his charisma shining through. The security guard looks unsure but nods anyway and walks off, throwing a glance at us over his shoulder.

'I'll tell your *wife* you had to leave,' Dad tells me with hatred in his eyes. 'I can't stand to be anywhere near you right now.' He stalks off back to Sarah's room.

CHAPTER 27

‹

'What do you mean my membership has been revoked?' I know raising my voice is a bad idea. I don't want to draw attention to myself, but the embarrassment of my swipe card not working has irked me.

'I'm sorry, sir, but it says here you are no longer a member of the gym. Was it not at your request?'

'Does it bloody look like it?' I ask the blonde woman behind the desk.

'Would you like to speak to management?'

'Yes!'

The young receptionist picks up the phone and speaks quietly into the mouthpiece whilst I keep watch of the gym floor for Millie leaving.

As Millie is refusing to take my calls and sitting outside her house is too obvious, I have taken to spending time in the gym to catch sight of her. Hiding in plain sight. It's a stake-out mission every time and puts a ton of stress on my shoulders in case I get caught, but seeing her is so worth it. I just need to know she's okay. And I need to get my dose of her or I'll lose my mind.

'Darren will be down in one minute.' The receptionist doesn't make eye contact with me and immediately turns away to occupy herself with something on her screen. Her cheeks are flushed.

As promised, Darren appears from the stairs behind me just moments later. 'Mr Briens,' he booms, reaching a hand out to shake mine. I ignore it and he drops it again with a squint in his eye. Good. He should be annoyed. This is no way to treat a paying customer.

'It's *Dr* Briens, and why can't I get in?' I demand, getting straight to the point.

'Would you like to go somewhere more private? This is a rather delicate matter.'

'No, I would just like to get this over with as quickly as possible. Just let me in. This is absurd.'

'I cannot do that, Dr Briens. I'm afraid we have had a number of concerns raised regarding your behaviour and we feel the simplest thing to do would be to remove your privileges.'

I scoff. 'You must have confused me with someone else. I've done nothing wrong.'

He cocks his head to the side and squints at me. His shoulders are incredibly broad, and his hands are the size of dinner plates. 'We have already confirmed the accusations on CCTV, Dr Briens. If you'd rather us get the police involved ...'

'What exactly am I being accused of here? I've broken no rules.' I double down, but I'm starting to feel a shift of nerves. There's no way he could know. I'm always so careful.

'Your behaviour has been inappropriate. Dr Briens. A number of members have pointed out that you don't come here to work out.'

I can't deny that. Not once have I stepped on a treadmill, and I haven't lifted a single weight. 'Maybe I just come here to clear my head. That's allowed, isn't it?'

'Yes, I guess so. But choosing to sit in the dance studio to watch women work out has made a number of people uncomfortable. We feel it is in the gym's best interests to terminate your membership.'

He doesn't know. I can fight this. 'What a load of shit. How do you know I am watching the women? I'm just getting some peace and quiet in the studios. I find looking over the gym motivating, that's all.'

His lip curls in distaste. 'We have footage of you pleasuring yourself, Dr Briens.'

I want the world to swallow me whole. I checked for cameras. I checked, goddamn it.

As if reading my thoughts, Darren says, 'Our cameras are strategically placed as people have a tendency to steal equipment. Now, I have tried to be nice, but I will not tell you again, you are banned from this gym and I suggest you leave now or I will call the police. I'm sure they'd be very interested to see the footage.'

I freeze, unable to make sense of what is happening. How have I stooped to such low levels? I'm not stupid; I know how lucky I am that Darren hasn't already gotten the police involved. In a bid to retain my dignity, I lift my chin that little bit higher as I march out of the gym, my cheeks burning hot with shame. And my eyes glistening with tears at the thought of losing all access to Millie.

The rain is freezing cold, dripping from my nose and ruining my suede shoes. Millie can't be too much longer. I hang back in the shadows around the side of the gym, not wanting to feel the humiliation of someone recognising me as the creep who lurks upstairs. Headlights flash past, temporarily blinding me and I blink away my blurry vision.

'Zack?' Millie's voice drifts over as if from the heavens above. 'What are you doing here?'

'We need to talk.' She's shivering. I need to get her warm before she catches her death. 'Come with me.'

She takes a step back and shakes her head. 'I've got nothing else to say to you. You should go.'

'Please, Millie. Just for a couple of minutes.'

'I'm done with you, Zack.'

'Please!' A sob catches in my throat, turning my request into a beg.

She pauses, looking at me quizzically. 'Zack, you need to hear me. I'm bad for you. I'm doing this for your own good.'

'You're wrong, Millie. Trust me on this. I can give you everything. You can't be bad for me if I am willing to give you every little piece of me.'

A shiver makes her jerk violently and she glances around the car park. 'Fine. You've got five minutes, but I'm not promising anything.'

I beam at her and shrug off my jacket, wrapping it around her bare shoulders before leading her to my car. As soon as we get in the car Millie turns her attention to cranking up the heat. She's confident in my space, I like that. I use her distraction to start reversing out of the parking space.

'Where are you going?' she asks, sitting bolt upright.

'I just want to talk to you, that's all.'

'We can talk in the car park. Stop now, Zack.'

'I'll stop when you hear me out. Please, just hear me out, Millie.'

I glance to my left and see Millie staring at me with pure loathing. 'Go on then. You've got five minutes before I lean my head out this window and scream.'

I drive around aimlessly, trying to think of how best to make her see sense. With Sarah out of the way in the hospital, this is my chance to take everything I want. Once I convince Millie that I am right for her, I can take my girls and run. Then, when divorce proceedings start, there's no judge in the country that will let a woman have custody of a child when she gets so drunk she can't even navigate stairs. I can get my happy-ever-after.

Millie takes the lead. 'Zack, what you walked in on before. Me and that guy. Just so you know, that wasn't me. I was acting out. I don't usually have random guys in my bed. The longer Dexter has been gone, the more confident I feel about him never coming back. And I guess I'm just acting out.' She shrugs.

Anger courses through me at the mention of our last meeting. 'It's okay,' I lie, eager to put that behind us. We need to look forward and focus on our relationship. Besides, she's entitled to make mistakes like everyone else, especially as she's hurting from her abusive boyfriend leaving her in such strange circumstances. It's no wonder her behaviour is so out of character.

'Though I must admit, I'm glad to hear he was some "random guy".' I force a smile, but she bristles. 'Millie, you have to understand what I have to say.' I rest my hand on her thigh, but she yanks her leg away. 'This is going to sound crazy, but I know, without a shadow of a doubt, that I was made for you. We are made for each other. I'm in love with you, Millie.'

She just stares out the window looking bored.

'Give me a chance and I can make you so happy.'

Sighing, she says, 'Zack, you're married. This is all just a twisted fantasy.'

'That's just it, I'm not married! Not anymore.'

'Oh, Zack. What have you done?' She drags her hands down her face.

'Sarah and I have agreed to separate. She will still live at home, but we're most definitely not together.' I wait for the smile I know will erupt on her face at my good news. But it doesn't come. 'Millie? Did you hear me? I'm a free agent, we can be together now.'

'You need to take me back to my car now,' she says, her voice harsh enough to make me look at her. 'Time's up.'

'No, we need to sort this out,' I tell her.

'Take me back now.'

I don't say anything. Why is she acting like this? Did Dexter mess her up so badly she doesn't know how to be happy?

'I know this is a lot to digest, but Millie, think about it. Think about what this means!' I don't bother to turn the car around like she requested. I know I can make her see sense.

'Take me back, Zack.' To my dismay, she sounds furious. Me leaving Sarah was supposed to be good news!

'Only when you agree to consider what I have to offer you. I can give you unconditional love, a huge home, money, safety. Anything you want.'

'But you *can't* provide what I want. You don't have it.'

'Tell me what it is and it's yours. Let me show you.'

'Take me back. This conversation is over.'

'No! No, it isn't. I'm not taking you back to that ridiculous gym. You should stay away from there, too.' My foot automatically presses harder on the accelerator and the car lurches forward. 'They kick good people out for no good reason,' I mutter under my breath, furious at the injustice of being banned.

She spins to look at me with squinting eyes and a tight jaw. 'Nooo,' she says, the syllable drawn out in disbelief. 'You're the guy?!'

'What guy?' My stomach churns nervously, anticipating what she's going to say.

'The guy everyone is talking about. The sick fuck caught wanking in the dance studio.'

'What?! Of course not.' But I can't stop the burn that rises from my neck to the top of my forehead, my embarrassment visible for Millie to see the truth.

'Jesus Christ, Zack. Why were you tossing off at the gym?'

I don't dignify that uncouth question with a response. We've gone off topic.

'Please don't tell me I've got something to do with it. Were you pleasuring yourself over me?' She sounds disgusted. Like my actions at the gym weren't the ultimate compliment.

I try a cheeky approach. 'Well, what can I say? You're an attractive girl.'

'Take me back. Now!'

'No!' My temper spills out of me and my foot presses down on the accelerator harder. We're sailing past shops and houses, lights blurring around the vehicle.

'Who the fuck are you? You're sick, Zack.' She places a hand on the door handle and I flick the locks in case she decides to jump out of the speeding car.

'Oh my God. You did kill Dexter. Didn't you? I doubted you at the time, but you seemed so nice, so genuine, and I gave you the benefit of the doubt. But you're a sick fuck and you killed him!'

'Not this again. I didn't do anything to him.'

'Oh, please. You're sick in the head, Zack.'

'No,' I whisper, unable to comprehend the twist in events. This was supposed to be a happy conversation. Life-changing.

Millie looks around frantically, her head moving wildly from side to side. I have no idea where we are.

'Please, take me back to my car,' she pleads now, on the verge of tears. 'Please Zack, if you love me like you say you do, you'll do it. I'm scared.' Her voice drops to a girlish whimper and my heart cracks in two.

I turn to look at her and see her skin is as white as the moon above us. Tears glisten on her skin. I feel awful. Releasing my foot off the accelerator, I let the car drift back to the speed limit.

'I'm so sorry, Millie. I didn't mean to scare you. I just wanted you to see me for who I really am.' I cannot stop my tears. I have never lost control like this before and the release is as cathartic as it is horrifying. 'I'm just a man desperately in love.'

She doesn't say anything. She just sits panting next to me; my breath is as ragged as hers. This isn't going to work like this. I need to approach this again when we're both in a calmer frame of mind.

I turn the car around.

Chapter 28

'Goodbye, Miss Perez. Do let me know how the trial goes. I have every faith in the justice system.'

The sweet Miss Perez says her goodbyes and leaves my office. I breathe a sigh of relief. Managing the office alone these last two weeks has been no easy feat.

With my head constantly spinning, I crave a slice of normality, but I can't do it. No matter how hard I try, I can only give my clients fifty percent of what they deserve and it isn't good enough. I shouldn't be here. I know I shouldn't, but with everything collapsing around me, I can't let my business collapse too.

Given that Chelsea told Sarah about my kiss with Millie, we both thought it best that Chelsea take some time out of the office for us both to cool off. With everything going on with Millie, I wasn't ready to tackle the Chelsea situation. Everything just feels too much right now.

Chelsea is back on Monday, so I'll face it then. For now, I just need to focus on keeping it all together. Especially with Sarah coming home from the hospital today.

I glance at the clock. Four o'clock. Miss Perez was my last client of the day, so I take a seat at Chelsea's desk and open her emails. I don't want to go home to see Sarah and there are over fifty unread emails, so I decide to tackle all of them tonight and hope Sarah has gone to bed before I get back. Helen is staying with us for a few days so I know Sarah and Georgia will be taken care of.

Despite everything, Sarah has been incredible these last few weeks. It's as if her fall was the wake-up call she needed. She has been positive, reasonable, and practical in making our separation work. From today, Sarah has given herself one month to find somewhere to live nearby so Georgia can spend time with both of us. She asked me if Georgia can continue to live with me until Sarah has settled into her new home and secured a job. Then we can arrange a more joint arrangement. Home life is all falling into place at last.

The lift pings open and I inwardly groan. I'm too tired to face an unscheduled therapy session right now.

'Chelsea?' I'm stunned to see her marching towards me with a smile on her face. She's wearing heels so high I worry for the state of her ankles. She's wearing what she terms a *power suit* and her lips are painted bright red, which tells me she means business. I immediately feel uneasy.

'Dr Briens,' she says, taking a seat opposite me. It's strange seeing her sit on the other side of her desk. Everything is topsy-turvy.

'How are you doing? I wasn't expecting to see you until Monday ...'

'I just thought we should talk before I return to work. Thank you for giving me the time off, by the way.'

I wave away her gratitude. 'I thought it best. I don't want to lose you and I wanted to do something nice for you. Despite what you did.'

I swear if a pin was dropped on the other side of the room, you'd hear it. Chelsea's smile vanishes and is replaced by a look of disgust.

'Despite what *I* did?' She sounds incredulous. I don't know what's happening. Chelsea must know exactly what I'm talking about. Her tattle tales caused a fight so huge I nearly killed my wife. That's all on her.

'We both know you told my wife, Chelsea. About my indiscretion.'

'No, no, no. I will not have you blame me for your mess. Or should I say *messes*.'

What is she banging on about now? Doesn't she know I have no patience left for women with a chip on their shoulder? 'I think you should leave here before we both say something we regret.'

Instead, she just smiles at me. A smile that knows far more than she's letting on. All of a sudden, I feel oddly exposed. 'We both know you have a bit of a thing for Emily O'Neale, don't we? The image of you two practically fucking is burned on my retina.'

'That's enough!' I yell, slamming the mouse I was gripping down onto her desk.

'But she isn't the only one, is she? How about Katie Bloxham, Sunita Sharma, and Cassandra Burke?'

She takes my breath away, opening wounds that have barely scabbed over. 'I don't know what you're talking about,' I say.

'Don't treat me like that. Like an idiot. Before I started here, your old receptionist got in touch with me to warn me about you. About how you like to take advantage of clients. She said you paid her to keep quiet.'

'As if I would do such a thing.'

'That's exactly what I thought. You seemed so nice. So sweet. I figured your old receptionist just had it in for you or something, so I took the job and all seemed fine. But then, after the whole Millie thing, I was super pissed off at you so I had a little rummage around your office. Tell me – why do you have a thong in your office, Zack?'

My stomach rolls. How dare she go through my things?

'And what about the rest of your little stash? Your trophies. Underwear, lipstick, a bejewelled mirror. I highly doubt they were yours. Am I right?'

No. This cannot be happening. My eyes flicker towards my office door that sits open, mocking me with the secrets it failed to keep.

Chelsea laughs. 'Your little keepsakes aren't in there anymore.'

I feel sick. I'm not ready to let go of my memories of the women I loved. 'Where did you put them?'

'Somewhere safe. And I intend to keep it that way.'

'What are you going to do now?' My fear is overwhelming. I want to run, scream, and roll into a ball and cry all at the same time.

'That depends on you,' Chelsea says.

I look at her. Chelsea has always been the image of professionalism, it's why I hired her. I admired her for it. And now is no exception. She's sitting bolt upright, her posture perfect. Her eyes do not stray from mine, not for one second.

'As you know, I'm getting married. And, given that you owe me for keeping your reputation intact, I think you should pay for the wedding.'

I can't help but chuckle. The way Chelsea has been banging on lately about her perfect day, her wedding will cost more than twenty thousand pounds. 'No, I can't do that.'

'You sure about that, Zack?'

Suddenly emboldened by Chelsea's ludicrous demand, I say, 'Chelsea, the underwear means nothing. It could belong to anyone. It's time you quit this charade.'

'Oh, please. They must be covered in DNA. I found *hair*, Zack. Actual human hair.'

Shit. I forgot I stole Sunita's hairbrush.

Shit, shit, shit.

Chelsea hands me a post-it. 'Here are my bank details. You've got until Monday.'

CHAPTER 29

The house is quiet when I storm in.

How dare Chelsea blackmail me after everything I have done for her? I gave her a job when she had abysmal work experience and terrible qualifications. I saw something in her and honed her into a fantastic employee. I paid for her to go on courses, taught her excellent organisational skills, and rewarded her handsomely. And now she's doing this!

How dare she?!

I pull open the fridge and take out the open bottle of wine. Pouring myself a glass, I listen out for Georgia coming down the stairs. I don't want her to see me gulp this back. I don't want her to think I'm as bad as her mother. There's no sound, so I empty the glass.

After placing the glass in the dishwasher, I head upstairs to see how Georgia is doing. She had a project due at school today and I want to know how it went. But her room is empty. Her bed is unmade and toys litter the floor. Everything looks normal. So, where is she?

I take a quick look in Sarah's room, but she's not there either. Maybe Helen took them back to hers?

I go to call Sarah but as I am tapping on the screen, something catches my eye. Sarah's wardrobe door is ajar. Just an inch or so. Something doesn't feel right here.

I step deeper into her room and open the wardrobe door. Every hanger is empty. They sway as if mocking me. I job over to her drawers which are empty, too.

I run back to Georgia's room, panic coursing through me. I check her wardrobes and drawers too – nothing.

'Fuck!' I scream out, running down the stairs to the living room. After everything that has happened to me lately, I can only assume the worst.

I open the cupboard under the TV and pull out the box that contains our passports. Only mine sits in the box, my face staring up at me. I look glum, like I always knew everything would turn to shit one day.

Tears spring to my eyes, a mix of fury and pain. She's gone. Georgia can't be gone. A roar erupts from my core. This isn't happening. This isn't fucking happening!

I march into the kitchen, completely unaware of my surroundings. I whack my elbow on the doorframe as I step past, but I ignore the pain throbbing from deep within the bone.

I try calling Sarah but the robotic voice tells me: *This number is no longer in use.*

Helen doesn't answer my call either and in a fit of rage, I throw the phone across the room. It hits the sink and lands with a crack in the cloudy water.

'No!' I gasp. That phone has all my contacts on it. I'm helpless if it's dead.

I should have known everything was going too well with Sarah. There's only one reason she would lie like that. Only one reason she would do this to me – she knows the truth. She knows I pushed her down the stairs.

The bitch played me.

Which means I cannot go to the police. There's nothing I can do to get my baby girl back.

A burning sensation pulses up my throat and I hurl up into the sink. Onto my phone. Great, more shit to deal with. I scoop it up and clean it on a nearby tea towel. It stinks, but I slip it into my back pocket.

Not knowing where to go next, I pick up my car keys and jog back to my car.

CHAPTER 30

Not knowing what to do, I swig on the bottle I picked up from the off-licence. The burn of the whiskey in my throat feels satisfying. It's the only thing that feels real right now.

I drive around aimlessly so I'm stunned when I pull up outside Millie's. She's like a magnet. A big fucking magnet. It seems my mood isn't improving the more I drink. I feel calmer for it, though.

Millie is out. Her car isn't in her drive. I imagine her out buying sexy new lingerie for her new lover and I have to blast the music in my car to distract myself from the pain in my chest.

I'll wait. The rain lashes down on the windscreen, the sound fighting against the sound of Jon Bon Jovi singing some drivelling ballad. I continue to sip on the whiskey and dial Sarah's phone again – nothing. Helen's number yields the same result. I don't know what else to do and the world is spinning, making me queasy.

I feel like I'm going to explode. Every one of my muscles is tense and aches. I shift in my seat and press my hands to the ceiling to ease the knots in my back. This is all an absolute joke. A bad dream. I'm one of the good guys, I don't deserve any of this.

I squeeze my eyes shut and let my mind drift back to Georgia's sweet face.

I cannot lose her.

Even if she isn't biologically mine.

My solicitor's words ring loud and clear between my ears:

'But the fact remains, Dr Briens, you're not on the birth certificate. I know you have raised your daughter from birth and I'm not saying getting full custody isn't possible, but no judge in the land will be on your side with Sarah being a present and capable mother. You're running uphill with broken legs. If I am honest with you, I wouldn't rock the boat. There's nothing stopping Sarah from challenging your access rights to the child and I can promise you, you'll lose that battle. You could lose your daughter.'

'But she's a drunk!' I shouted, losing my temper.

'Do you have any evidence of that? Any doctor's notes? Any testimonials?'

I thought I had testimonials. I have been planting Sarah's alcoholism into my family's minds for years. Yes, I exaggerated, but I needed their help. I needed them to help me prove that Sarah is an unfit mother.

But no one believed me. No one saw what I saw.

Sarah's infidelity was embarrassingly obvious. The dates didn't line up. There was no way Georgia could be mine.

I left. Of course I did – I'm a man of honour. But when I turned up at my parents' house with my suitcase, Dad turned me away.

He told me to man up and stay with my wife. For better or worse. And in return, I get a daughter to love.

So I trudged back with my tail between my legs and hatred in my heart. I stayed with Sarah through the pregnancy, driving her to appointments and sitting outside in the car. Waiting anxiously outside whilst she screamed through the birth.

As I was supporting Sarah, Dad supported me. Together we sourced a location for my practice; he helped me fill out the licensing paperwork; he even paid everything to help me get started.

I knew what he was doing. He was modelling what a good dad looked like, so I could be the same.

And it worked. The second I held Georgia in my arms, I knew I would love her forever.

Sarah and I never talked about Georgia's biological father. I didn't want to know and I knew if we looked the raging bull in the eye, it'd all be over. Wounds would tear open so deep there'd be no coming back from it.

The years slipped by and we lived in not-so-blissful ignorance. Until the night I pushed Sarah down the stairs.

The bitch deserved it.

Then, I thought I'd figured it all out. By pushing Sarah down the stairs, I opened my own eyes to the possibilities. It showed me what I was capable of.

That was my trial run. When Sarah woke up, I saw it as a second chance. I would end this mess properly. Sever ties with my wife one final time, then live happily ever after with the two girls I love.

This was supposed to be my happy ending.

I shake off the urge to cry and my vision wobbles. I chuckle. The irony isn't lost on me. Sarah ruins my life and what do I do? I turn into her. I drink to numb my pain. I can almost see the appeal now.

CHAPTER 31

Another fifteen minutes pass and just as I am contemplating driving to the nearest off-licence for a refill, Millie's car comes roaring around the corner. She spots me sitting in my car as she pulls into her driveway and a scowl creases her brow.

I stagger over to her, not bothering to shut my car door behind me. 'I thought I told you to leave me alone?' she calls over to me through the rain. She takes a proper look at me and cocks her head. 'Are you drunk? Jesus Christ, Zack, you look steaming.'

'I'm not drunk,' I reply, but I can even hear the slur in my speech. 'Okay, maybe I'm a little tipsy.'

She moans at me and raises her hands in defeat. 'For God's sake, Zack. Go home and sort yourself out. If you keep harassing me, I'll have to call the police.'

'You wouldn't do that to me. I'm your therapist.' The last word spits out. Even I know how ludicrous that sounds. I've been a pretty terrible therapist to Millie.

'Wouldn't I? I'm pretty sure they'd be fascinated to hear what you did to Dexter.'

I groan. 'Not this again. I thought we were done with this. I didn't do anything to your pathetic boyfriend.' Spit flies from my mouth with the insult and lands on Millie's arm. She wipes it away with disgust.

'Please just go.' Millie turns and walks to her house. She fumbles with her keys, offering me a chance to catch up. 'I just need to talk to someone. I need to talk to *you*. I've been there for you, it's the least you could do.'

'It's your fucking job, Zack! I paid you! Don't act like you were doing me a favour.'

She pushes the door open and runs inside, but I'm too quick for her and slip in behind her. 'Zack, no. Get out.'

'Not until we talk,' I tell her. I reach out to touch her soft skin, but she slaps my hand away. I've lost my daughter. I will not lose Millie, too. With Millie by my side, I know I can claw my life back. I will not leave here until I win her over.

'Right, that's it.' Millie turns away from me and reaches into her handbag. She pulls out her phone and jabs her finger on the screen. 'Police please,' she says into the receiver.

'No!' I shout, smacking the phone away. It lands on the stairs and tumbles down, the screen cracked in one corner.

'Zack!' she yells. She goes to pick up the phone, but I kick it away where it hits the skirting board. The screen completely shatters and the phone dies.

Fear sweeps across her delicate features and the guilt of being the cause of her terror makes me feel sick. My desperation is too high, and I can't seem to stop myself. The whiskey is making me bold. I should've started drinking years ago; maybe I wouldn't be in this mess right now. 'Sorry,' I tell her, trying to make it sound like I really mean it. 'I'll buy you a new one.'

She stares right in my eyes, her fury burning a hole in my heart. There's a moment of calm as we stare at each other, trying to make sense of the situation before she darts forward, shoving me out of the way as she reaches for the door. Her aggression takes me by surprise and I stumble drunkenly, tripping over Millie's dropped handbag. In what feels like slow motion, I crash into the side table.

'Millie!' I call out, but she pulls open the door to leave. I'm about to lose her forever. Everything is broken. I'm losing myself in a world I no longer recognise.

Without thinking, I throw my foot out, catching Millie on the back of the knee. To my horror, she falls heavily and her head smashes into the door.

'What the fuck is going on here?' a voice calls out. A man steps inside the ajar door and rushes over to Millie's aid.

She takes one look at him and blanches. 'Dexter.'

CHAPTER 32

'Dexter!' Millie gasps again. 'Oh, thank God!' She drags herself into an upright position and falls into his arms. I can't help but notice he doesn't pull her close to him. The embrace is awkward, like an invisible wall separates them. He pushes her away.

I can't help but feel a little pleased. It is far from a grand reunion.

Using the table as support, I pull myself up. The alcohol running through my blood feels more potent than ever.

Dexter checks Millie over, holding her at arm's length. 'I'm not staying long.' He says to her with a look of pure loathing. He doesn't wait for a response before turning to me. 'And who are you? Are you her new conquest? You have to be careful, she'll lure you in with open legs and trap you.'

I bristle I never slept with Millie. Only in my imagination.

Recognition sweeps across Dexter's face. 'Wait. You're the one who was in here that day, weren't you? Creeping out of here like a sad little puppy.' He laughs. 'Don't worry, I would've been pissed at having someone snoop around my house, but I was so happy. I thought she'd found herself another plaything. Someone to take the attention off me for a little while. Sorry mate, but you weren't the first. And you certainly won't be the last.'

My lip curls over my teeth. 'I'm her therapist,' I say, straightening my torso, and brushing down my shirt. I raise my head, feigning sobriety and confidence. There's no way this monster is going to get the upper hand here. No matter how drunk I feel. 'And I know everything about you. Everything you did to her.'

Millie nods at me defiantly. Probably glad to have me here to fight in her corner.

He looks at her with a creased brow. 'Is that so? And what is it I do to you? What are you telling people about me?' He pushes her away, but she stays rigid, her chin raised in defiance. I'm proud of Millie. She's come such a long way since our first therapy session.

'Where have you been, Dexter?' she asks him, a twisted smile playing on her lips. 'It looks like you've been in the wars. What a shame.'

His mouth gapes open and his left hand grips his right wrist. I notice for the first time his cheeks are hollow like he hasn't eaten properly in weeks and his greasy hair is pushed back, the oil slicking it into a wild mess. 'I just came to get my stuff, Millie. I didn't think you'd be here.'

'Yet, here I am,' Millie goads. 'So, what's your plan now?'

Dexter moves to go upstairs but Millie cowers and screams with exaggerated pain. Dexter didn't even touch her. 'Please don't hurt me!' she squeals, but the smile doesn't leave her face. She feigns hiding behind her arms, but her laughter betrays her.

What is going on?

Dexter shakes his head in disbelief. As he steps back, he stumbles on his left leg but manages to remain upright. 'No, Millie. Please don't do this.'

'What? Protect myself? Oh yes, I bet you hate that. You like me weak, don't you? Begging. Pathetic. Well, not anymore. I'm done with you.'

'Okay, that's enough, Millie. Let me go in peace and I won't breathe a word of all this. Let me go.' Millie laughs manically, firing every single one of my nerves. Dexter continues. 'Please, Millie. I'm not putting up with you anymore.'

She steps in front of him, blocking his way. I feel like I'm not really here. It's like watching a drama on TV unfold in front of me. I feel sick, the alcohol burning the back of my throat. I lean back against the wall to brace myself.

Dexter winces as Millie touches his arm. 'Please don't touch me!' he barks, but she doesn't remove her hand. Her nails whiten as she squeezes harder.

'Where are you going, Dex?' Her voice is tense and deep, it's as if a new Millie is bubbling to the surface. Her timidity is gone. She's a lioness, ready to fight back. I feel my pride swell.

'Get your hand off me.'

'You don't call the shots here, Dexter. Remember? Now, tell me where you've been.'

'I'm going to get my stuff and I am leaving.' His tone has matched hers now and I can hear the aggression she's had to live with for the last year. It's peeking through his weak façade. 'Now let go of me!' He pushes her. Hard.

My fist smashes into his cheek with such unexpected force and I cry out in pain. My knuckles feel crushed from the impact. But shockingly, Dexter barely flinches. He looks like the fucking Devil as he glares back at me.

There's a breath between us before he launches into attack mode, jumping on me and pulling me to the ground. His punches hit hard against my jaw and stomach as he pins me down with his knees. He smells like sweat, the stench stifling my breath. I can't think straight, and I lie on the floor like a fucking idiot, taking the abuse. Absorbing the pain Millie has suffered at the hands of this man. If he's hitting me, he's not hitting her.

Through my drunken stupor and Dexter's punches, I frantically glance around me. My eyes catch Millie's. She's calling for me. Finally, she sees me for who I am. Her protector. Her future. I feed on her desperation and draw strength from it. With a mighty roar, I push Dexter away. He claws at me, a man possessed, but I've got more to fight for. Love is a stronger force than hate.

Dexter falls back and clutches his face. He's panting. 'We shouldn't be fighting. We're on the same side.'

I take my chance and launch myself on top of him and thrust my knuckles into the bridge of his nose. I hear it crack and blood gushes from his nostrils.

'Zack!' Millie calls out again. My name on her lips fills me with a huge sense of pride. I'm doing it! I'm protecting her! 'You can stop now.' Her voice is stern, and it catches me off guard, making me pause to look at her. I'm confused. I'm doing this for her like I have done everything for her. Why is she angry with me?

Without warning, Dexter grasps my throat and squeezes, pulling my attention back to him. Millie can't possibly want me to stop hurting him. Surely, she can see this man is deranged?

Heat rises into my skull as I desperately seek the breath I need to survive. I can't. I can't fucking breathe. The dizziness returns tenfold, and my eyes roll back into my head. My hands flail, completely disengaged from my brain. My fingers graze something hard and cold, and my eyes fly open. Through the spots piercing my pupils, I spy a vase on the table and will my fingers to grasp it. It feels like weeks pass before

I manage to grab the ceramic base. It's heavy and from the clinking sound as I drag it off the table, I realise it's full of loose change.

I don't have long. I know I have one chance at this before I pass out. My vision blackens and my imagination gifts me the image of Millie gazing at me adoringly. I know I'm dying.

Millie's face is replaced by Georgia's. Her perfect little face flitters behind my eyes and an energy pours from me. I need to see Georgia again.

I smash the vase into Dexter's skull. The sound of the vase breaking mixes with the sound of cracking bone. A cacophony of death.

CHAPTER 33

Millie's laughter rings through the air.

I'm sitting on the floor looking to the ceiling, gasping for air to draw life back inside of me. My throat burns as I gulp down the cold life source. I place my hands on my head to open my lungs up, and my bleeding knuckles sting as my fingers straighten.

Dexter lies at my feet. His eyes are open but glazed over. It's like his life has been sucked out of him, leaving behind a body without the soul. It's eerie, and I itch to close his eyes to make him stop looking at me.

Blood pools over the floor, the puddle edging towards me at a rapid pace and I watch as it edges towards my shoes. I am too stunned to move away. It's like none of this is real. As if I am watching this from outside my body.

Millie continues to laugh, pulling me back to reality. She's in shock. She's hysterical.

'Millie,' I croak, barely making a sound, and she doesn't hear me over her cackle. I force myself to cough in an attempt to get her attention. 'Millie!'

She lowers the volume, but laughter continues to spill out of her. Her cheeks are flushed and her eyes shine brightly. 'Oh, Zack. You should have seen yourself. Acting like a hero. All macho.' She raises her arms and flexes her biceps in demonstration of my machismo.

I don't get the joke. 'Millie, you're in shock.'

She laughs harder then. 'All you men are the same. You think you know everything and you think you're the absolute dog's bollocks, yet you're so fucking simple.' She desperately draws in a breath through her laughter. 'You're all so ... pliable.'

What is she talking about?

She continues. 'You're like the pieces on a chessboard. You're all fucking pawns and so easy to manipulate.'

It's nonsense. Millie hasn't played me. Not for one second. This is Dexter's doing. He's made her think she's in control by vanishing, when actually he was the puppet master the whole time, pulling her strings. 'I saw the bruises.'

'What, like this one?' I watch in disbelief as Millie clenches a fist and brings it to her eye so hard that she knocks herself backwards.

I gulp. Now he's dead, she's lost her mind. Did Millie really hurt herself? Surely not. I have seen some pretty concerning cases in my time, but this takes self-harm to an all new level.

'No, Millie! Stop it.' Her eye is already red, the beginnings of a bruise starting to form.

Her laughter stops abruptly. 'Don't you tell me what to do.'

'No, I didn't mean it like that. We just need a clear head. We need to sort this out.' I gesture towards the corpse that's still staring up at me with accusatory eyes.

'*We*? I think you'll find this is a *you* problem.'

My eyes dart between the two of them. I might not be intoxicated any longer, but my near brush with death has left me just as confused.

'Millie, you have to help me. I ... I killed him ... for you.' The words feel electric on my tongue, as if saying them forces the truth of the situation to sink deeper into my brain. I would feel guilty, but right now, all I can feel is panic. I killed a man.

'No, Zack. I won't help you.' Her bluntness cuts through me. 'I knew the second I met you, you'd help me, but I never expected it to work out so well. It has been such fun!'

I shake my head. I have a sneaky feeling she isn't talking about therapy.

'I mean, you were my get-out-of-jail-free card, had Dexter found the balls to go to the police. I never thought you'd kill him. I thought you were too much of a pussy. Apparently not.' She squats down and leers at Dexter. 'Poor Dexter, you never did learn how to behave. And I never did figure out how to get you under control. But my God, did I try.'

My tongue feels heavy in my mouth. 'What do you mean? What are you talking about?'

She laughs again. Only this time her laughter contains no joy. It's pure malice. She stands up. 'You really think this piece of shit can bully me? Please.' She pulls her leg back and kicks him in the head with full force. The brutality of it takes my breath away once again. *I'm going to tell the police,'* she says, mocking Dexter's Scouse accent. *'Please stop. Please, Millie. Stop hurting me. I'll do anything.'*

Her cruelty makes my skin crawl, but my curiosity gets the better of me. 'You abused him? Everything was a lie?'

She shrugs. 'What can I say? I like to play.' She stamps on his face, caving in a cheekbone, her stiletto heel leaving a sickening hole in his face next to his open mouth. She pulls it out with force, dragging him a few inches towards her. 'And Dexter was my toy. For a while, he was a good boy. Kept my home to my high standards. Made me orgasm when I needed the release. And he took his punishments like a good boy whenever he displeased me.'

This can't be happening. Millie is the monster.

'But, then the little bitch got all whiney. Started complaining to me about being unhappy. Like he didn't understand how lucky he was to even breathe the same air as me. You know, don't you Zack? You know what an honour that is?'

I can't bring myself to look at her. Is it fear that averts my gaze? Revulsion? No, she's just Millie. I know her.

This isn't really happening. This is a stupid drunken dream. Georgia is mine. Dexter is alive. Millie isn't insane. But the metallic smell emanating from Dexter's draining body shatters my illusion. This is all very real. 'Where were you keeping him?'

'Who?'

'Dexter,' I snap, my tone harsher than intended.

She bends so her face is inches from mine. She presses her index finger into my chest. 'Don't you take that tone with me. And for your information, I didn't keep him anywhere. I have no idea where he went for all these weeks. I figured he'd just faked his own death to get away. A coward's exit, if you ask me.'

But that doesn't make any sense. Why would he just come back? Why would he try so hard to break free only to come wandering back into the lion's den?

All I know for certain is I need to get out of here. I try to stand, but it takes three attempts before I can push myself upright.

Millie watches me with glee in her eyes, enjoying my pain. 'Where are you going?'

'I need to go.'

'Go? Don't you think you should sort this mess out first?' She gestures at this poor man's body like it's a pile of dog shit.

She's right of course. I can't just leave here. My DNA is splashed all over this place. All over the man I killed. And I have a sneaky suspicion Millie isn't going to help me get out of this.

I shift my weight onto my left leg, then back to my right. I brush my hand through my hair. Decision made, I glance around the room and see it resting on the floor by the living room door. Bending makes me nauseous, but I scoop my phone up off the floor where it fell out of my pocket during the fight. I dial the number.

The phone rings for an age before he picks up, his voice horrifyingly weak. 'Dad? I need your help.'

CHAPTER 34

D ad pulls up in a car I don't recognise with a look on his face that shows he means business. I go out to greet him before he meets Millie. There's a fire in his eyes that terrifies me.

'Dad,' I start, but he shuts me down with a punch to the face. I stagger backwards.

'No, Zack. You do not get to worm your way out of this. You got yourself into this mess, you will not bore me with your sob story.'

I stand clutching my jaw and watch as Dad pulls on some gloves and storms over to Millie who is leaning against the doorframe looking out at us with a look of amusement. They exchange a few words and Millie gestures inside. She turns to me with a smirk when Dad steps inside. I jog over to join them.

'Fucking hell, Zack. What have you got yourself into?' It's a rhetorical question and I hang my head. The shame I feel after being duped by Millie is immense.

'What do I do?' I ask him, my voice barely audible over the thundering rain.

Dad's eyes bore into mine. 'I think you should just leave. You've made a big enough mess.' His breathing is laboured and there's a yellow tinge to his skin. I have never seen him look so old.

'Dad, you can't do this alone.'

'Of course I fucking can. There's life in this old dog yet, you know. Go and get some frozen peas on your face. I'll deal with you later.' Dad pulls his hood up, burrowing into the fleece. His eyes are sunken and he looks malevolent tucked into the shadows of the fabric. He claps his hands together. 'Right, Zack, you fuck off.' He gestures at me. 'I'll be in touch.'

'Go on,' Millie says, taking my hand. I pull away from her cold skin. 'You should go and leave daddy to fix this.'

'What are you going to do?' I ask her. I don't want to leave her with Dad. I want him to hear the full story from me, not Millie's dark tongue.

'She's staying here!' Dad barks. 'I'll need her help. But you need to go. You'll only hinder things here.'

Dad's glare is uncompromising and with trepidation, I leave.

I can't return home to my empty house and I feel like I'm about to burst into a billion pieces. Everything that has happened in the last twenty-four hours is all too much and I can't hold it in anymore. The cracks are rupturing.

I would do anything to go back to my life as it was just a few months ago. I was getting by. I had a business I was proud of, a daughter I worshipped by my side, and I was blissfully unaware of Millie's existence. What have I become?

I can't imagine how bad my marriage must have been for me to feel such hatred for Sarah. She wasn't that bad. She *is* a good mum to Georgia, I just refused to see it because I was hurting. Because I was terrified my relationship with Georgia would end. I was at Sarah's mercy and I hated her for it.

I know now that I should have made more of an effort with Sarah. We could have been something. We could have at least been an incredible team, bringing up Georgia to be a strong, confident, and loved woman. Instead, we dragged her down into the depths of our mess.

I head home to change out of my blood-covered clothes, but the house feels vast and soulless. It's suffocating. I can't be here. So I decide to head to my parents' house to await news from my dad.

Mum opens the door with a sweet smile on her face, oblivious to what her husband is doing right now. 'Hi Zack. Are you okay, dear?' Her eyes widen and she gasps at the state of my battered face. 'Oh, Zack, come in. I'll get the medicine box.'

I can tell she is too afraid to question me in case I tell her something she doesn't want to hear. I imagine she thinks Aaron is involved in this and she'd hate to think her boys are fighting. I stomp into the living room. She goes into the kitchen and I can hear her rattling around in the cupboards and the tinkle of the ice machine.

I glance at myself in the mirror over the hearth. My hair is pulled in all directions. My face is bruised, and a thick purple line rings my neck where Dexter tried to squeeze the life out of me.

'I thought you'd need something strong to drink,' Mum says, eyeing my reflection over my shoulder. She hands me a measure of whiskey, the scent making me feel sick. She gets to work dabbing my face with a cold, wet cloth. 'Zack, you have me worried. What's happened?'

'Nothing, Mum. Nothing for you to worry about, anyway.'

Her eyes widen but she doesn't say anything. I inwardly cringe as I place the whiskey down on the mantle, remembering what trouble I got into last time I was drunk. Was that really a few hours ago? It feels like both a lifetime and three seconds ago.

'Okay, dear.' She sounds so small, like a little mouse. She holds a towel filled with ice to my lip.

Almost two hours later, the front door slams shut and I jump up to greet Dad. Mum doesn't even glance away from the TV. She's far too absorbed in *Antiques Roadshow*. Or too lost in thought about me and what mess I have gotten myself into.

'Dad! In here,' I call out to him. I hear him wheezing before he even steps into the room, and he stumbles through the door.

'Graham?' Mum stands and pulls him over to the sofa. 'Good God, what is going on with you two today? You both look awful.'

'I can't speak for him.' Dad gestures at me. 'But I'm okay, Theresa. Is that drink going free?'

I hand Dad my untouched whiskey, now watered down by melted ice.

'Maybe you should go to bed. I'll call the doctor.'

'For fuck's sake, Theresa. You're always fussing.' Mum recoils in shock. Dad breathes deeply. 'Sorry love, I'm just tired. How about you go to the chippie? Fish and chips is sure to perk me up a bit.'

Mum hesitates, but leaves as instructed.

'How'd it go?' I ask him, like I'm asking about his day at work and not about the disposal of a corpse. A man I killed.

'It's sorted. That's all you need to know.'

'What did you do with ...'

'No, boy. You don't get to ask any questions. The less you know, the better. And you have to promise me this: you are not to go anywhere near that house or that woman ever again. She doesn't exist to you. You hear me?'

I nod my head but I don't mean it. Dad sees right through me.

'I mean it! You've cocked up big time, Zack. It's about time you did as you were told.'

'I know, Dad. It's just ...'

'No!' His shout ricochets off the walls, making me wince. 'You might act like you're the big guy but you're a fucking mess, Zack. And I've had enough of it.'

'Has it occurred to you that I'm a mess because of *you*?' I yell. 'I never felt good enough for you. You were so hell-bent on making my sham of a marriage work, you pushed me into a box so small I couldn't fit. Isn't it any wonder I screwed up?'

'Bullshit. You're a big boy, Zack. You make your own choices, not me.' Dad's lips twist into a grimace and his eyes squeeze shut.

'Dad? You okay?'

'Well, Millie was the last time I help you, Zack,' he wheezes.

'Last time? I've never asked for your help, Dad.'

'Bullshit! Who put the deposit down on your house? Who paid for your business? Who do you come running to every time you fuck up?'

'I never asked for those things! You practically threw money at me and I couldn't exactly refuse – no one refuses you. You get whatever you want.'

Dad coughs weakly and slumps back into the sofa. The whiskey he was clutching drops to the floor. 'I just wanted to help. I wanted a better life for you.'

'What do you mean?' My pulse is racing and the rush of blood through my brain is audible. Dad's eyes close, making my fury soar. 'Better than what? Aaron's? Don't get me started on him. Why do you hate him so much, Dad? What did he do for you to treat him so badly?'

Dad clutches at his chest. 'Call an ambulance,' he mutters.

I watch him, trying to decide what to do. I want answers. Everything has been spiralling and for the first time in a long time, the ball is in my court. Dad will be fine until I get some answers.

He looks at me with bloodshot, desperate eyes. 'I just don't love him like I love you. It's why I killed them all, son. I wanted the best for you.'

Dad is clearly unhinged in his panic. 'Killed who?' I take my phone out of my pocket but I don't make the call.

'The women you were seeing. You needed to be with Sarah. You needed to be a good man, and they were stopping you.'

The realisation dawns and hits me like a tonne of bricks. Dad stabbed Katie, strangled Sunita, and locked Cassandra in a room. Then he let their abusive partners take the fall.

He slumps to the floor. I watch him as his breathing becomes more laboured. He's clutching his chest. His eyes don't leave mine, they're begging me to help him. But I can't. I can't do that.

Then all goes quiet.

'Dad?'

Dad doesn't speak. He doesn't open his eyes.

I watch as he takes his last breath.

Only then do I dial an ambulance.

CHAPTER 35

Minutes tick by, each agony. Each mocking me. *You killed him too*, they taunt.

Mum returns from the chip shop. The smell of cooking oil and vinegar wafts through the house. Before she has even slipped her shoes off, the flashing lights of the ambulance pull up outside the house.

Mum's scream when she enters the room will stay with me for the rest of my days. Her face immediately drains of colour as she runs towards the love of her life. Squawks of disbelief pour out of her. 'No. No. Graham! No!' She kneels beside him and throws her body over him, trying to pour life back into him with an embrace.

The rest is a blur. People in uniform come and go, taking Dad with them. Mum sobs into her sleeve. I say I'll follow the ambulance, but I can't. I already know he is dead. And there is no way I can look Mum in the eye.

As soon as the ambulance peels away, I run.

The world is spinning around me. I'm delirious. Spots form before my eyes and I shake them away, refocusing on the pieces of my life.

'Millie!' I call out again. I hammer on her door and to my relief it pushes open with ease. Dusk is dulling my sight and so I step into the house, running the back of my hand over the wall for a light switch.

I don't know why I'm here. My life is just so disastrous and I have a craving for answers. Millie's confession has left me so confused and I need to know what happened to Dad when I left him here. What did she do to him to make him come back in such a state? This is all her fault.

All of it.

My foot presses on something soft and the carpet emanates a squelch sound. 'Shit,' I mumble. Dad didn't clean Dexter's blood. What was he thinking leaving the evidence here?

My hand sweeps over something cold and I flick on the lights.

I step back, gasping at the sight. Dexter is still lying on the floor, untouched. His skin is grey and his eyes stare at the ceiling, all life behind them wrenched out of him. I cannot fathom why he's still here. Dad said he sorted this out.

'Millie?' I call out. I slip off my shoes and throw them through the open door into the rain. I don't want to tread blood everywhere.

I scan the downstairs of her house. Nothing. I head upstairs, careful not to touch anything and follow my instinct into the bathroom. I struggle to catch my breath as I push open the door with my elbow. There's something wrong here, something evil. It chills my bones, and I cannot explain it.

The small light over the mirror is on, casting ominous shadows across the room. The shower curtain is pulled across the bath, and I know the source of my unease lies behind it. I have just witnessed my dad die in front of me. It's no wonder I'm tense. I shake off my paranoia and pull back the curtain.

I scream. The blood is stark against the white enamel of the bath. My breath catches in my throat as I stare at her pretty face, her eyes closed with a look of serenity. Her sweet mouth is open just a little, her lips still pink enough to kiss. She lies naked, her breasts resting on the red-stained water. Her arms rest on the side of the bath, both wrists sporting thick, deep cuts where her life spilled out of her.

'Millie,' I whisper. 'Oh, Millie. What did I do?'

CHAPTER 36

I haven't left the house since the will reading last week.

Dad's last words constantly play on my mind, taunting me with the truth of his betrayal. I see him now. I see that because I didn't fit his mould of a perfect husband, he felt it necessary to walk into my life and take the lives of women who truly didn't deserve any of the pain life threw at them.

My anger towards my father is so intense, it burns. Yet my guilt at the part I played in his death is immense. To add to all that, my sorrow at not having seen my daughter in over a week is killing me.

And I killed Dexter. I am no better than the man I called my father.

I sit here now, a knife bouncing from hand to hand as I contemplate why I would bother to go on. Why not just end things here? I have nothing else to live for. The walls of what was once my beautiful home are closing in on me. I'm surrounded by misery and the pain of it is encouraging me to slide the tip of the blade over my wrists.

The police have been sniffing around.

'Can we ask your professional opinion on Emily O'Neale?' A tall, young officer asked me, her glasses perched on the tip of her nose.

I told them the truth: how Millie was a troubled lady trapped in an abusive relationship. Or at least, it was the old truth. The truth I understood and took for granted. And my client files corroborated that.

'Did Emily ever show tendencies toward self-harm?' The police officer then asked me.

'That's exactly why she came to see me. She frequently harmed herself.' Again, the truth, be it a little twisted.

That seemed to satisfy the officers who went back to work, declaring Millie had killed Dexter in self-defence before taking her own life. A tragic ending I can't deny.

It seems Dad did an excellent job at clearing up after Dexter's death. Well-practised, I guess. There was no reason to question anything. I'm grateful the police have more work on their plates than time to properly investigate anything in depth.

Once again, Dad gets off scot-free, the abusive partners I have in my case notes all evidence supporting false conclusions. And I continue to walk free.

I know I don't deserve this. I know I should be punished for the part I have played. I led innocent women to their deaths. It was a fate I saw all too often in my work or at conferences where truths were whispered about clients. Women die all the time at the hands of the men they love.

Only this time, it was my hand by proxy.

I killed Dexter, though. That was all me. And I watched my dad die.

I grasp the knife handle and squeeze the metal beneath my palm. It's warm and comforting.

I've lost it all. Despite paying Chelsea's blackmail money, my business has still crumbled. My behaviour and cancellations led to a tirade of bad publicity on social media. My daughter is God-knows-where, most probably being turned against me by Sarah, who quite frankly has every right after I pushed her down the stairs.

I'm balancing on a tightrope that can wobble at any minute. Everything can come crashing down. I could lose my freedom as well as everything I love. Both Chelsea and Sarah have good reason to make that happen. I close my eyes and press the knife tip to the delicate skin on my wrist. The skin breaks and I watch with fascination as blood beads around the tip of the knife.

The doorbell rings, making me jump. I drop the knife and it slips to the floor, landing with a gentle thud on the carpet.

'For fuck's sake,' I mutter under my breath. I close my eyes and take deep breaths and wait for the visitor to leave. Blood trickles down my arm.

But, whoever is at my door is persistent. They ring the bell again, and once again just a second later. With exasperation, I get up from my seat, my muscles fighting against my desire to move.

'Who is it?' I call through the door.

'It's me, Aaron. Let me in.'

'Not right now. I'm busy.'

The door handle rattles. 'Unlock the door, Zack. We've got things to talk about.'

I press my forehead against the wall. I'm not strong enough for this.

'I'm not leaving here until you let me in. And I can be pretty vocal when I don't get my way.'

Sighing, I unlock the door and walk away, allowing Aaron to let himself in.

'Wow, you look like shit,' he tells me.

'What do you want?' I lean against the wall, exactly where Sarah cracked her skull.

'It's the funeral tomorrow. Are you ready?'

I shrug. I know I told Mum we could have it here, but I haven't given it a second's thought since I made that promise.

'Look, Zack. We've got to keep it together. For Mum.' He thinks I'm falling apart over Dad. I guess he's right, he just has no idea *why*.

My eyes meet his and for the first time I look at him properly. It looks like he has aged a decade in the last week. His eyes are bloodshot and his mouth droops, heavy with untold burden. 'You okay?' I ask.

'As well as I can be.'

I look at him more carefully. A truly broken man stands before me. There's simply no way Dad's death could do this to him. They didn't have a tight enough bond. 'Talk to me, Aaron. Please.'

He looks at me with raised eyebrows and sighs. 'Dad was a judgemental bastard. I never got the chance to make him proud.'

I nod, pulling up a stool and taking a seat. My body aches from the recent trauma. 'He was a nasty piece of work, that's for sure.'

Aaron cocks his head to the side but doesn't ask me to explain myself. 'He hated me. He never let me just be ... *me*.'

I think of Dad's desperation for me to make my marriage work and I grunt in agreement. Only rather than withdrawing his love, like he did with Aaron, he suffocated me with it. 'Why did he hate you so much? What went on there?' I finally have the balls to ask now Dad is dead. I was too afraid before, in case my involvement pissed Dad off. I didn't want to disappoint him.

Aaron presses a finger to his lips. I imagine the truth finally coming out feels strange. 'Remember when you all came to see me when I passed basic training?'

I nod. It's the memory captured in the photo on Mum's mantlepiece.

'Well, Dad got all pally with my sergeant. They spent hours talking.'

I nod along. Dad always liked to talk to the highest-ranking person in any room, be it military or civilian. I always assumed he just liked to talk to someone he thought was at his same level.

'Well, apparently my sergeant made a joke about me, about who I really am, in front of Dad. And that was it. Dad told me to quit. And I did. You never say no to Dad, right?'

I chortle. 'That's true.'

'He said he wanted to "fix" me.'

I restrain myself from asking questions. This is Aaron's story to tell. He should feel able to tell it in his own way. Plus, if I speak now I'm afraid it'll break the spell between us and Aaron will run.

'Zack.' His eyes lock with mine and I draw on my therapist training and inject sincerity into my gaze. 'I'm gay,' he admits and looks away. 'I'm sure you can imagine how Dad took the news.'

I swallow down my shock. Poor Aaron. For the first time in years, I can appreciate everything he's said and done. The acting out. The look of loss scarred on his face.

Dad was disgustingly homophobic. He would turn off the TV if two men dared kiss on the screen. He'd cross the street at the sight of men holding hands. He once hurled abuse when he saw a man propose to his boyfriend. It was embarrassing. But it was part of Dad. I never agreed with his opinions, but I knew I couldn't fight them either, so I turned a blind eye. I had no idea his hatred was directed at my brother, too.

'Dad always knew,' Aaron says. 'I think he thought the army would straighten me out. Hanging around with "real" men who craved sex from women. So you can imagine his reaction when he found out I'd been caught kissing a chef behind the cookhouse.'

I soften at Aaron's revelation. My poor brother, locked away. Shutting his true self inside. Forced to lie to present an image that satisfied my father. It's no wonder Aaron shut himself out of the family. 'Aaron, I'm so sorry. I had no idea.'

'Then Dad's plan worked,' Aaron chuckles. 'When I was a kid, he used to coach me on how to behave straight. Date girls. Don't dress too campy.' He laughs, but it's full of pain.

We sit in companionable silence. Aaron's admission has stripped away all animosity between us. 'Did anyone else know?'

'Just Sarah.'

I force down the annoyance that is threatening to spill over. I always knew Sarah and Aaron had a strange friendship, but I assumed they were bonding over both being a pain in my arse. I had no idea Aaron was opening up his vulnerabilities to my wife. Maybe she isn't so bad after all.

'Are you seeing anyone?' I ask eventually, changing the subject.

He winces. 'I was. But he left me.'

'I'm sorry.'

He waves a nonchalant hand at me, but he fails to hide the tears that glisten in his eyes. 'He was damaged. It came as no surprise when he disappeared. Especially when I spent so long hiding him away like a dirty secret. He deserved better than me.'

'Want to talk about it?'

Aaron's blue eyes meet mine. 'I've tried to talk to you. So many times. Each time I'd bottle it and make up some shit excuse about needing money.'

I hang my head in shame. 'I'm so sorry. I had a lot going on. And I was a shit brother.'

'I think we're both guilty of that,' he says. He scrapes a nail over a mark on his coat. 'He was treated like crap.'

'Who?'

'My boyfriend. My ex-boyfriend. We were never an item, not really, but we got along and there was this strong attraction there, you know?'

I nod. I know exactly what he's referring to. I felt it all too often with the women Dad killed.

Aaron continues. 'We used to meet in secret in a rough pub in town, somewhere I knew none of Dad's mates would go. He'd open up to me. And I to him. He told me how his ex treated him like absolute shit. Eventually it all got too much and he came to me for help. He stayed at mine. You should have seen him, Zack. He was too terrified to leave. It was fucking awful. But I loved him. So damn much.'

I tut. 'I guess men are as shit to other men as they are to women.'

'Nah. That's just it, Zack. He was with a woman. She was a fucked-up bitch, that's for sure. Zack. Dexter deserved so much better.'

'Dexter ...?'

'Yeah. His ex did so much damage. I kept telling him to just face her. Go and get his stuff from hers and move on with his life.'

Not knowing where to look, I just nod along with his words.

'Anyway, I think I pushed him too hard and one day he said he'd sort it all out. I wanted to go with him, but he wouldn't let me. Then when I got home from work that day, he'd left me.'

Tears pour down his cheeks and he heads into the dining room to cry in private.

I am too stunned to move. Aaron was in love with Dexter.

And I killed him.

'Zack? What's this?'

Shaken out of my guilt, I stumble into the dining room to find Aaron holding the knife I almost used to take my life. I shrug. Like an idiot.

'Zack. You're not doing this.'

I feign confusion. 'I don't know what you're talking about.'

Aaron looks down at my wrist and I realise a small trickle of blood has dripped over my hand where I previously pricked my skin. It has dried and is starting to form a crusty red track across my skin.

Aaron's sobs return with vigour. 'No, man. You're not doing this. You're my big brother. I fucking need you!'

'A shit brother,' I sob in return.

'Well, yeah,' Aaron snorts a sad laugh through his wet face. 'But believe it or not, I need you now. And what about Georgia? She needs her dad.'

I look at the floor. How dare Aaron be nice to me after what I did to Dexter?

'Please, Zack. Promise me.' His plea is barely audible but it stabs me in the heart. I owe this man everything. I will do whatever he asks of me.

'Okay,' I tell him. 'I promise.'

Aaron pulls me in for a tight hug, slapping me on the back.

I'll take my secrets to the grave if it means protecting my family.

CHAPTER 37

I run my hands down my jacket, smoothing out the creases. My suit could have done with a dry-cleaning, but with Sarah gone, I failed to take it in. It'll have to do.

'You look smart.' Her voice calls over to me from the doorway.

I spin to see my wife staring at me. To see her standing in my room stuns me into silence. I always imagined this moment would come with violence; with a need to make her pay for what she's done to me.

'Helen's outside before you think of doing anything you'll regret,' she says, as if reading my mind. She waves her phone at me and I see it's calling Helen's phone, the line connected.

'I didn't hear you come in,' I say stupidly.

She cocks her head at me, and her shoulders visibly relax. 'That's not the welcome I was expecting. I thought you'd be raging at me.'

'Oh, trust me, I am. But I've been through a lot lately. I'm just glad to see you're back.'

Her eyebrows crease with concern. 'I had to come. I heard about Graham. I'm so sorry for your loss.' Her voice cracks but I don't have time for her tears.

Speaking of my loss, I ask her, 'Where's Georgia?'

'At Helen's.'

I nod, my muscles tense from fighting the urge to jump in the car and drive to my daughter.

'I got a letter from your dad's solicitor,' she tells me.

'So you know about the trust fund for Georgia?'

Dad was a bastard in death as he was in life. Always controlling. Always diverting his efforts to his fucked-up values, no matter how miserable they made everyone else.

Dad's will was insightful. Being a constant source of disappointment, my brother got nothing. Fine. What surprised everyone the most was that I wasn't in his will, either. I didn't get a penny.

I tried not to let it bother me. I don't want his dirty money. But I can't help but wonder why. I thought me and Dad were close, so for him not to consider me feels like a slap in the face. Like our relationship meant nothing to him all these years.

My mother got the bulk of his wealth, of course. And he left Georgia an eye-watering amount of money in a trust fund. According to the trust conditions, Georgia will receive a quarter of a million pounds when she turns eighteen. The catch? Sarah and I need to be living together as husband and wife and not have taken another partner. That's twelve years locked in a marriage with Sarah. Twelve years of utter misery for both of us.

Sarah nods. 'What do you want to do?'

I turn to face her. 'What do you think is best?'

'Zack, the way I see it, another twelve years of this marriage could do more damage to our child than missing out on a bit of money ever could. I think we should divorce.'

It's an interesting notion. I thought the same, but something niggled at me. 'No,' I say, turning back to fiddle with my tie. 'We owe it to Georgia to do everything we can to get her what she deserves. We've been unhappily married all these years. I think we owe it to her to at least try.'

'Our marriage is poisoning her, Zack. Surely you can see that.'

'Which is why we have to make more of an effort. Look, I'm not saying it'll be a conventional marriage. It's obvious there will never be any love between us. But, we can live together as man and wife without the love of man and wife.'

I see her step towards me in my peripheral vision. She's now inches away from me. Her perfume is sickly sweet and gathers in the back of my throat. 'You really think we can do that?'

I laugh and turn to her. 'We can try. For Georgia's sake.' And if it means I get to keep her in my life, it will be worth every second of it.

She shakes her head. 'I don't think I can do that though, Zack,' she whispers.

'Please, Sarah. I can't lose you both, too.'

She looks at me with large eyes and touches the back of her head where her hair is still short from her operation. She pales. 'You scare me. I worry about what you'll do to me.'

I break down as what I did to Sarah comes back to me in crashing waves. Every tiny bit of pain pours out of me. I crouch on the floor and let the sobs come in thick wails. 'I'm not a bad person, Sarah. I'm not. I'm really not.'

Sarah hesitates before crouching down next to me. She presses a hand on my shoulder and I realise she is crying, too. 'We've made a pretty big mess of everything, haven't we?'

I nod. 'No, I have. I've ruined everything.' Snot bubbles out of my nose. 'I'm so sorry, Sarah. I will never hurt you ever again. I'm not a bad person.'

'I know, Zack. I know good people can sometimes do bad things. I know that more than anyone.'

I continue to sob, grateful that Sarah understands. Or is at least trying to. I know my actions are unforgivable, but if she can just give me a chance to show her how sorry I am, she'll forgive me. She has to. I will not have Sarah take her away from me again. My little girl is all I have left to live for.

CHAPTER 38

My dad's coffin enters the mouth of flames, delivering the justice he deserved.

As angry as I am to learn of his actions, I still mourn the man I admired. The man who brought me into this world and gave me a career, a home, and family values (even if I struggled to abide by them). Dad had high expectations and a messed-up code of ethics but, if I dare to shine a positive light on it, he stood his ground and lived by his morals one hundred percent. I admire that. I just wish he had felt differently.

Even in his death he continues to make me suffer – tying me to a woman for the sake of the one thing left I truly love. But I know that I have brought nothing but pain to Georgia's life and I need to repent. I will stay with Sarah until I can provide everything that little girl deserves.

Sarah sits by my side, tears stream down her crimson face. The tissue she is clutching is sodden.

I haven't yet spoken to Aaron this morning. And I glance over my shoulder to see him sitting in the back row. He is staring at the floor, refusing to watch my dad's body turn to ash. I can't imagine how he's feeling. Free, I should hope.

He's kept his true self locked away for the sake of my father's beliefs. I hope he's brave enough now to reveal his true colours and live a happier, more fulfilled life. Maybe there's hope for us yet.

The officiant concludes the service, everyone stands up, and a stifled mumble sounds out around me.

'You okay?' Sarah whispers at me.

I can't talk to her right now. As much as I want to, I can't face her. My emotions are too raw and I'm scared I'll spill the truths that need to be locked away forever. No one can know what Dad did. If his secrets come out, then mine spill too, and I have just got my daughter back. I shake my head at Sarah, refusing to meet her eye.

Sarah coughs and looks pointedly over my shoulder. I turn around to see Mum staring at us. 'Zack, dear, can I have a quick word?' Sarah takes the hint and walks away. 'I would appreciate you and Sarah keeping your differences to yourself, just for today.'

'You don't need to worry, Mum. I'm sure we can stop fighting for just one day.'

I meant it as a lighthearted joke, but Mum's eyebrows crease in a look I have never seen on her face before. She looks livid and there's a terrifying glint in her eye that takes me aback. She looks around, seeing who is in the room with us. 'I know how hard it is to keep your dad's secrets – I have been doing it for years. But I swear to you, you breathe a bad word about him today, you so much as taint anyone's memory of him, and I swear to God I will make your life miserable.'

I take a step back. Who is this woman? 'Mum? What secrets?' Does she know I was there when Dad died?

'Don't you dare try and bullshit me. It's your fault your dad is in that coffin. You chose your whore over what was right, and Graham had to pay dearly. *I* had to pay dearly.'

She jabs at my chest with her finger and I lean back in shock. 'I didn't do it, Mum. I didn't kill him.'

'Zack? What did you just say?' Sarah is standing by the door, her hand to her mouth.

'Of course I didn't!' I shout at Sarah. 'What are you doing here?'

She's turned a horrifying shade of white. 'I know when you're lying, Zack. Your lips move.'

'I didn't kill him.' I whimper.

Mum is sneering at me. 'I didn't say you did,' she spits. 'I wasn't talking about that. But now, I'm not so sure.'

My mouth shoots open. My eyes flit between the two women in my life: one representing love, the other hate. Only now that's blurred. I can only feel their hate. I slump down onto a nearby chair. I'm utterly confused.

Then it dawns on me. She knew what Dad did for me. To Katie, Sunita, Cassandra. Even Millie. And now I've dropped myself in it.

Sarah marches over to me and leans in so that her face is inches from mine. 'You truly are a piece of shit. You killed him, didn't you?'

'I didn't kill him! Please back off. This has nothing to do with you.'

'But this has everything to do with me!' she screams. 'You killed Georgia's father!'

Silence rings loud. It's like I'm submerged and it's suffocating me. This cannot be happening. Sarah is lying. 'What did you say?'

But Sarah doesn't say anything. Her lips tremble.

My sight is blurry, but I can make out Mum slipping her arm through Sarah's. There's no anger there. No surprise. Mum knew about Dad and Sarah, too. About Georgia.

'Mum?' I sob. 'Tell me it's not true.' I shake my head, forcing the world back into focus.

I see Sarah stomping out of the room without so much as a backward glance.

'It's true,' Mum sighs. 'It happened just one time. With Sarah, anyway. Your Dad had a wandering eye when drunk. But he only ever had love for me. He was a devoted husband, really.'

'How did you live knowing that? What is wrong with you? How dare you keep me in the dark?'

'You think it was easy? It was hard, but I managed to find it within myself to forgive him and we all agreed that you wouldn't be strong enough to do the same. And that didn't feel fair to Georgia.' She pulls her handbag strap further onto her shoulder. 'You were her daddy, not Graham. He's too old to father a little girl, it didn't feel fair.'

I'm weeping like a little child.

'So, we set you up in a house, with a career. Everything we did was for you, all of it.'

'Why did he want me to stay with Sarah so much? Why ruin my life like that?'

'He knew if you two went through a messy divorce, truths would start to spill. Devastation tends to loosen one's lips.'

'And you knew about my affairs? What Dad did to stop them?' I choke on my cry and cough it out.

'I knew. And no matter how many times we stopped you, you kept going back for more, didn't you? You couldn't keep your penis to yourself. Like father, like son, I suppose.'

'And you didn't care? You didn't mind being married to a murderer?'

'No. Because I believe in the sanctity of marriage. I will stand by him until my dying breath. And now, I believe in the sanctity of yours.'

CHAPTER 39

ONE YEAR LATER

Moving through grief is never a linear process. The last year has seen me leap into a bottomless pit of despair, only for me to crawl my way out before diving straight back in again. It has been a long, lonely journey and it's only lately that I feel like I can breathe again. Even if it's just a little.

I sign off the letter I am writing and place it in the box with all the others. There are eight in there now. I didn't know what to say at first. What do I say to the girl I raised as my own, not realising that she's actually my half-sibling? It's a notion I will never truly get over. As much as I love Georgia, I will never be able to look at her the same again.

Not that Georgia knows this. Sarah never returned after the funeral. She vanished. Not even Helen knew where she went.

So, I started writing letters. Each one telling Georgia she is loved. Each one letting her know that I am not a bad man. And one day I might give them to her. When I track her down.

I'm not in any hurry to find them. I can't face Sarah right now. I can't let desperation guide me anymore. I need a clear head and the only way I can achieve that is to heal first.

I tuck the Peppa Pig pyjamas in the box, too. A sob escapes me but I swallow it down. There's plenty of time for that in bed later. I can't cry now.

Millie still crops up in my thoughts regularly. I was a fool to fall in love with Millie. I don't know what I was thinking. I was a man looking for a way out in all the wrong places. A caged animal will either completely give up all hope, or lose their mind. Shamefully, I was the latter.

My part in Millie's game is a curious one. She used me to cover up her sickening treatment of Dexter, I know that. But why seduce me? Why pull me even deeper into her game? I may never know the true answers, but I have a good idea: control. Millie had to manipulate everyone around her. True narcissistic personality disorder.

I should have seen it. Things could look so different right now if I had just done my job properly and diagnosed Millie straight away.

It goes without saying that I no longer practise as a therapist. For now, I mark assignments for university students. It's low income but I share the household bills now, so I get by.

Aaron is still mourning Dexter and that guilt will never leave me. I have many regrets, but taking Dexter away from Aaron is my biggest. He deserves happiness.

My brother was a victim of my dad's bigotry and since Dad's death, Aaron is starting to come out of his shell. He's kind, gentle, and hilarious. He's the brother I always wanted. And, given what I took from him, I'd do anything for him in return.

'You okay, bro?' he asks me now.

'Yeah, just lost in thought.'

Aaron grabs the remote and turns on the TV. Since moving in together, we've found a mutual love of soap operas. He loads up last night's *Coronation Street* so we can catch up on Steve Barlow's latest affair.

We have a strange relationship. We're clearly both healing, which puts a strain on things but we're healing together, tightening our relationship, thread by thread.

And that's all I can do right now. Piece by piece, I will fix my relationship with my brother, Georgia, possibly even Sarah.

And maybe one day I can heal myself, too.

LIKE WHAT YOU READ?

There's more!

For free books, competitions, news on the author and general silliness, sign up to the mailing list at subscribepage.io/ejJ56y

Or join in the fun on Facebook by searching for '**C.L. Sutton Author**'

Alternatively, drop me an email at **hello@clsutton.com** and I will endeavour to reply to you personally.

Thank you from the bottom of my heart

It means so much to me that you have taken the time to read my book. A monumental amount of time, effort, and love is poured into every book written and I think I speak for all authors when I say we are grateful for your support.

If you want to help give my book a boost, please consider leaving a review and recommending me to your friends. It's a HUGE help.

Printed in Great Britain
by Amazon

52932241R00124